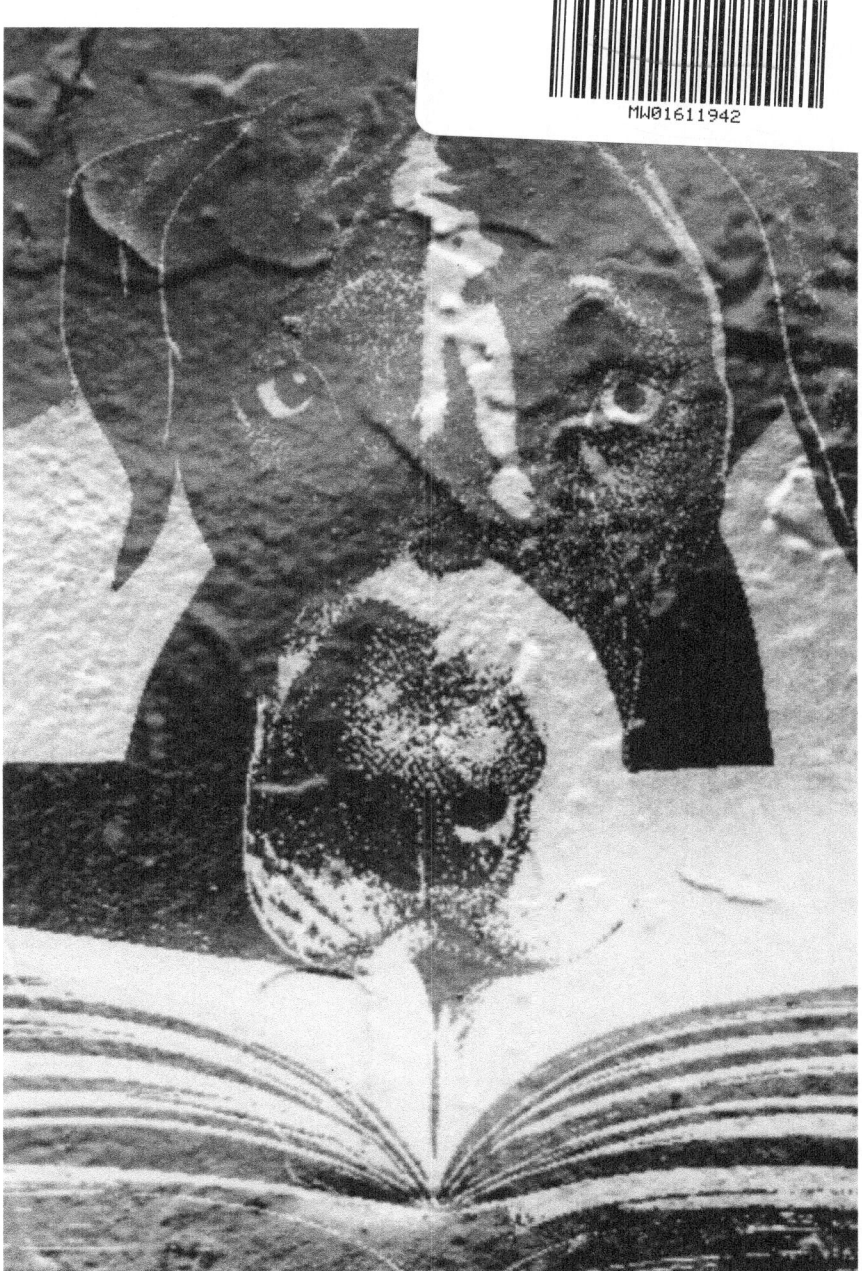

1

# GENIUS SPECIES
# CAMERON SIMMONS

# Table of Contents

........................................................................................1

Prologue ........................................................................6

Part 1 .....................................................................10

1 ....................................................................12

2 ....................................................................35

3 ....................................................................45

4 ....................................................................55

5 ....................................................................73

6 ....................................................................86

7 ....................................................................107

8 ....................................................................144

9 ....................................................................153

10 ..................................................................165

11 ..................................................................173

Part 2.................................................................203

12 ..................................................................205

13 ..................................................................232

14 ..................................................................272

15 ..................................................................285

16 ..................................................................313

17 ..................................................................327

Epilogue...........................................................355

# PROLOGUE

Jane was lost in thought, her mind wandering as she watched the raindrops dance on the glass pane of her window on this gloomy day. The sensation of her fingertips grazing the cold, smooth surface of the window made her feel connected to the outside world. The rhythmic sound of raindrops tapping against the glass created a melodic symphony that resonated within her.

A knock on the door interrupted her peaceful daydream, signaling the mail carrier's arrival with a package in hand. The knuckles rapping against the door resonated through the hallway, a sharp, distinct sound that cut through the quiet. The anticipation of what awaited her on the other side excited her heart.

Months have passed since her husband, John, vanished, leaving her trapped in her thoughts. Hungry for human connection, Jane's anticipation grew as she hastened towards the door, her hand extending to grasp the cool, metallic doorknob. The touch of the smooth, polished surface sent a gentle tingle up her arm, igniting her curiosity. Upon opening the door, fresh air caressed her face, carrying the intoxicating scent of petrichor—the earthy perfume of rain-kissed soil.

"Package for you, ma'am," the mail carrier announced, presenting a modest-sized box wrapped in earth-toned paper. The package felt substantial in her hands, the weight of it comforting and intriguing. She could feel the slight resistance of the tape holding the wrapping paper together as she carefully accepted the package.

Retreating to the sanctuary of her living room, Jane settled onto the plush couch. With hands trembling slightly, she began to unwrap the package, her fingertips gliding over the rough texture of the manilla wrapping paper.

Jane was met with warmth and energy as the last layer of wrapping fell away, revealing its contents. A vibrant Great Dane puppy emerged, its sleek fur glistening with droplets of rain. The puppy exuded a lively presence, its wagging tail creating a gentle breeze that brushed against Jane's skin. She reached out, feeling the softness of the puppy's fur beneath her fingers, savoring the furry texture that invited her touch.

Unaffected by the downpour, the puppy leaped towards Jane, his wet tongue greeting her face with exuberance. The sensation of his wet tongue against her cheek was an unexpected burst of coolness, a refreshing touch that awakened her senses. The sound of his excited panting filled the room, a joyous melody that drowned out the murkiness of the day.

The animated behaviors of the puppy momentarily distracted Jane from the cruel reality of her husband, John's, inexplicable disappearance. It was a sensory experience that grounded her, reminding her that there was still beauty and love to be found, even amid uncertainty.

As Jane embarked on a journey to unravel the mysteries surrounding John's disappearance, Dash, the lively Great Dane, became her steadfast companion. Together, they navigated a world of danger, betrayal, and unexpected alliances.

Through it all, the touch of Dash's fur, the scent of petrichor, the sound of his panting, and the taste of his wet kisses provided solace and strength, vivid reminders of the richness that could be found amidst life's uncertainties.

# PART 1

# 1

Jane was stunned when her missing husband, John, presented her with a Great Dane puppy. Although she wasn't a dog person, something about the pup's goofy walk and innocent eyes melted her heart and broke her defenses.

Jane's mind whirled with confusion, surprise, and concern as she stared at the unexpected package delivered to her doorstep. Her heart raced with worry and curiosity, wondering who would send her a container, especially one containing a live creature.

Carefully, she approached the box, feeling a rush of unease and intrigue. As she peeled back the layers of packaging, the distinct scent of fresh wood shavings and the faint aroma of puppy fur filled the air, intertwining to create a unique and strangely comforting smell.

Suddenly, a chorus of muffled whimpers reached Jane's ears, growing louder and more urgent as she unveiled the contents of the package. The cacophony of high-pitched yips tugged at her heartstrings, filling the room with an undeniable energy and life.

Her eyes widened as she focused on the tiny, wriggling bundle of fur nestled among the packaging. Its soft, downy coat tickled her fingertips as she reached down to scoop it up, feeling the warmth and heartbeat of the puppy pulsating against her palm. The delicate weight of the creature in her hands sent a jolt of tenderness through her veins.

As Jane cradled the puppy close to her chest, she couldn't help but notice its tiny body's rhythmic rise and fall, the gentle vibrations of its contented purrs resonating against her skin. The sheer innocence and vulnerability radiating from the puppy filled her with a mix of protectiveness and awe.

Thoughts raced through Jane's mind, a jumble of questions and emotions intertwining. "Who would send me such a precious gift? What does this mean? Is it a message from John? Or could it be a mistake?" Her mind spun with scenarios, each more fantastical than the last, as she tried to make sense of the unexpected arrival. "How did you survive in there?"

At that moment, Jane knew that her life had taken an unforeseen turn that would demand strength, compassion, and resilience. Holding the puppy close, she whispered, "Well, little one, it seems you and I are on this little journey together."

Dash was a sweet blend of awkwardness and charm. Its oversized paws tripped over itself in eagerness, and its floppy ears seemed to have a life of their own. His coat was as soft as a cloud, inviting her to bury her hands in its warmth.

Its eyes, a hypnotic blend of warm caramel and rich chocolate, held an almost human innocence. They sparkled with youthful curiosity and a deep longing for affection. This silent plea tugged at Jane's heartstrings in a way she hadn't expected.

As Jane read John's note, she was overcome with emotion by the beautiful curves of his handwriting, causing tears to well up in her eyes. Each written expression of his love was a powerful reminder of the depth of his feelings, which proved to be almost too much for her to handle.

As Jane read the note and felt the warm presence of the puppy, she couldn't hold back her emotions. Her tears weren't just a sign of sadness but a blend of feelings, including love, surprise, and a growing fondness for the giant canine that had unexpectedly come into her life.

Seeking solace, Jane turned to her Great Dane, Dash, who cozied up to her, providing genuine comfort she hadn't experienced since John's departure. Together, they opened the note.

*"My dearest Jane, I do not know how long I have been gone; if you are reading this now, I have passed away and left you with grief and pain. I am so sorry, my love; hurting you is the last thing I want to do. You are the best thing that has ever happened to me, and the day you said 'I do' was the happiest day of my life. As you can see, I have left you a puppy, a Great Dane named Dash. I have always been fond of Great Danes; he could keep you company. My*

*love, I would have given anything to be able to be there with you now but know that wherever you are, I am watching over you, your guardian angel. I want you to find happiness in my absence, and I want you to live a long and meaningful life.*

*With love,*

*John"*

In the quiet solitude, Jane folded the handwritten note, its creases sharp and tidy, before tenderly placing it atop the polished surface of her well-worn nightstand. Her new companion had already claimed his spot on the bed, sprawling across what was once John's side.

Jane perched herself on the edge of the bed, her mind fluttering through an avalanche of thoughts and memories. She allowed herself several minutes of this contemplative silence, her gaze fixed on the dimly lit wallpaper John had picked out.

She reached out and flicked off the bedside lamp. The room was a comforting cloak of darkness, the inky night wrapping around her like a soothing blanket. Jane surrendered to the awaiting arms of sleep, her heart heavy but hopeful for the dawn of a new day.

She awoke to the harsh grip of a frigid morning, the chill seeping into her bones and amplifying the stiffness in her limbs. The nagging ache in her back was evidence of another night spent tossing and turning. Six months had passed since John's disappearance, and the elusive shadow of sleep continued to taunt her, denying her a restful night.

The police's commitment faded, and the search for him dwindled. The once-bustling investigation had grown cold, leaving a void of unanswered questions and shattered hopes. Life moved forward, but the absence of his presence lingered like an unspoken ache.

John ventured out into the world with purpose and determination on that fateful morning of his disappearance. But as the hands of time ticked away, the minutes turned to hours, and he failed to show up to his workplace. A shared unease settled upon his coworkers, their concern intertwining with a growing sense of premonition.

The police, compelled to gather information, descended upon his workplace with a cloud of questions. As his coworkers were interviewed, the air crackled with tension, their words dissected for any semblance of truth. Whispers of marital discord between him and Jane invaded the conversations, a thread wading through the fabric of their lives.

The investigators, hungry for resolution, fixated on this narrative, concluding that he had escaped the turbulent confines of his marriage. Yet, a lingering uncertainty plagued their assumptions even as they clung to this explanation.

It was undeniably peculiar for someone to abandon their entire existence, not just a job but also cherished belongings and the connections that had once defined them.

John's absence resonated through the office walls, creating an eerie silence that filled the emptiness left in his wake. Once adorned with the trappings of a familiar routine, the empty desk now stood as a solemn reminder of his mysterious departure. Colleagues exchanged knowing glances, their eyes mirroring the unspoken question that danced upon their lips: *What happened to him?*

The truth lay buried beneath layers of speculation, a riddle waiting to be unraveled. The case, once propelled by urgency, now languished in the shadows of uncertainty. His absence whispered secrets and untold stories, leaving a haunting vacancy that refused to be filled.

Jane left the bed and went to the bathroom, each step mimicking the drumbeat of her loneliness. Catching a glimpse of herself in the mirror, she was met with a haunting reflection — a haggard face, haunted by fatigue, framed by unkempt hair, and underscored by dark circles, like sorrowful shadows carved under her once vibrant eyes.

The downpour of a scalding shower cloaked Jane, providing a brief respite from the weight of her thoughts. As the water cascaded over her, its steady rhythm echoed through the bathroom, drowning out the haunting whispers of John's memory. The steam filled the air, carrying the scent of lavender from her favorite shower gel, a soothing aroma that momentarily eased her troubled mind.

As Jane dressed, she felt the familiar sensation of her clothes against her skin. The soft fabric rustled and caressed her, creating a comforting sound that offered a brief respite from the intrusive thoughts of their last conversation, which played in her mind on repeat.

John's absence created an insurmountable void, transforming her once-ordered world into a fragmented puzzle, its jagged edges cutting deep into her soul. The weight of their shared memories, once a source of comfort, now pressed heavily upon her heart.

Their love story had blossomed within the halls of their high school, weaving together a youthful romance into a vibrant tapestry of marital bliss that spanned a decade. Laughter, dreams, and love interlocked their lives, creating a sanctuary in the world's chaos. They were more than spouses; they were kindred spirits, best friends, and pillars of support for one another.

Yet, the harmony they had once enjoyed began to falter under the strain of change when John accepted a position cloaked in strict government privacy. The transparent window into each other's lives was replaced by a foggy haze, a shroud of secrecy that cast long and unsettling shadows over the sanctuary they had built.

Jane grappled with this new reality, her heart torn between understanding and frustration. She longed for the familiar comfort of knowing every detail of John's life, as they had once shared.

However, the privilege of that intimacy had been replaced with cryptic gestures, evasive explanations, and an underlying tension that hummed in the background of their interactions.

Jane exuded a natural grace that defied her modest stature, standing at an average height with an air of elegance that captivated those around her. Her hair, a luminous cascade of golden-brown strands, was meticulously styled, each curl and wave a testament to the care she bestowed upon herself. Her beauty, though understated, stemmed from within, a radiant embodiment of her strength and resilience.

Distinct in her charm, Jane naturally avoided the world of social media. Real-life conversations held a far greater allure for her than the confines of online chats. When it came to fashion, she refused to follow trends, instead opting to wear what truly resonated with her unique style. Her wardrobe became a canvas, a reflection of her individuality and self-expression.

Jane was well acquainted with the harsh realities of mental illness, carrying the weight of anxiety as a constant companion throughout her life. She relied on anti-anxiety medication, a tangible reminder of her inner struggles. Like invisible storms, panic attacks would descend upon her without warning, engulfing her in a whirlwind of fear and leaving her gasping for breath, their impact profound and all-consuming.

Jane evolved into a creature of hypervigilance, always bracing for the next onslaught, her senses sharp, alert for the slightest hint of impending danger.

One haunting memory etched deep into her mind was a chilling instance of her stepmother's cruelty. Jane was imprisoned in a closet stretched for days when she was six. Her recollection of the experience was an instinctual montage of intruding darkness, a cruel heat that clung to her skin, and a thirst that gnawed at her insides with a savage intensity.

She cried out for help until her voice was a croaky whisper, unheard and unanswered. Her stepmother's chilling justification— that this was retribution for Jane's defiance—haunted her in the silence.

From Jane's perspective, the closet mutated into a timeless hollow where she was left to the mercy of her terrified imagination. Her mind, starved of sensory input, began summoning grotesque monsters that lurked in the shadows, their phantom breaths prickling against her skin. She wobbled on the edge of sanity, threatening to consume her whole.

The nightmare finally came to a shattering halt as Jane's father, his heart pounding in his chest, pushed open the door to the dimly lit room where his daughter had been cruelly confined. The sight that greeted him was beyond comprehension, a horrific tableau etched into his memory forever.

His eyes widened in disbelief as they fell upon Jane's withered form, now reduced to a fragile shell. Her delicate frame bore the unmistakable evidence of unspeakable torment.

Once smooth and unblemished, her skin now resembled a canvas of suffering—a patchwork of deep, purplish bruises and jagged scars that marred her innocence. Each mark told a story of her pain, a haunting witness to the cruelty she had faced in the shadows.

As he closed the distance between them, the stench of despair hung heavy in the air, mingling with the faint sound of Jane's labored breaths. Her frail body, a fragile vessel teetering on the precipice of existence, bore the weight of severe dehydration and malnutrition.

Every shallow rise and fall of her chest was a desperate struggle for survival as if her spirit clung to life by sheer determination alone.

At that moment, an overwhelming surge of emotions engulfed Jane's father. The horror that mirrored his daughter's own eyes etched lines of agony on his face, his expression a mirror of the torment he felt inside. The weight of guilt and love collided within him as he grappled with the devastating realization that he had failed to protect his precious child.

With a strength born out of desperation, he cradled Jane in his trembling arms, a mix of tenderness and urgency guiding his every movement. Time seemed to blur as he raced against the clock, every second an eternity in his desperate quest to save his daughter's life. Adrenaline coursed through his veins as he carried her, her frail warmth against his chest as a flickering flame of hope amidst the darkness that had consumed them.

Through the blur of tears, he navigated the complex corridors of the hospital. Doctors and nurses, their faces a mix of shock and compassion, sprang into action as they witnessed the harrowing sight before them.

As Jane was whisked away into the whirlwind of medical intervention, her father's mind was consumed by a singular thought—protecting his wife.

In a selfless act of misguided loyalty, he resolved to shoulder the blame for the unspeakable horrors inflicted upon their daughter. Little did he know that this decision would seal his fate as the swift wheels of justice began turning with an investigation that left no room for doubt.

And so, as the weight of guilt settled upon his shoulders, Jane's father found himself engulfed by the cold embrace of prison walls—the price he paid to shield his wife, who had played a part in their daughter's suffering.

The thought of that horrifying day cast its long, chilling shadow over Jane. The phantom sensation of the closet's claustrophobic embrace still lingers. Therapy offered a degree of relief, but the wounds of her past refused to heal completely. To cope, Jane had retracted from the world, erecting solid walls around herself, her fortress against the relentless assault of pain.

After the traumatic incident in the closet, Jane's parents, her father, and stepmother, decided to end their marriage. Despite this, her stepmother continued to fulfill the role of Jane's guardian, offering to care for her.

However, everything changed when Jane spoke to the social worker about her father's innocence during an unannounced visit. This conversation revealed compelling evidence that exonerated him from involvement in the alleged abuse. As a result, her father was released on probation, allowing him to rebuild his life and regain the trust of his loved ones.

At age fourteen, Jane embarked on a hunting expedition with her father, eager to deepen their connection and unravel the tales surrounding her biological mother. As the sun rose, casting a golden glow over the wilderness, the air was charged with anticipation and the faint scent of damp earth.

Jane gradually drifted away from her father's side in the early morning stillness, unknowingly straying into foreign hunting grounds. Suddenly, the deafening crack of a gunshot shattered the silence, echoing through the trees. Time seemed to slow as pain surged through Jane's body, her young arm seared by the bullet's burning path, blood pulsating in a terrifying rhythm.

Alone in the sterile hospital room, her heart pounding in her chest, Jane grappled with a potent mix of fear and desperation that seemed to consume her entire being. The cold, clinical surroundings only heightened her sense of vulnerability, amplifying the weight of the situation she found herself in.

As the days passed, Jane's mind became a battleground of emotions. The uncertainty of her prognosis loomed over her like a dark cloud, casting a shadow of doubt on her future. She clung to every thread of hope, desperately seeking reassurance that her young life would not be cut short.

The persistent waves of pain coursing through her body reminded her of the fragility of life. Each breath felt like a victory, a small feat over the unseen forces that threatened to overshadow her spirit. In those moments, she found solace in the presence of dedicated medical professionals who tirelessly worked to ease her suffering and guide her toward recovery.

Yet, even as Jane progressed, the haunting memories of that fateful day persisted. They invaded her dreams, vivid flashes of the ordeal she had endured, leaving her shaken and unable to articulate the depths of her trauma fully. The psychological scars ran deep, and the journey to emotional recovery would be just as challenging as the physical one.

As time passed on from this point, Jane became acutely aware of the emergence of panic attacks in her life. During this period, her internal struggles reached a tipping point, causing her mental and emotional well-being to suffer. The weight of unresolved trauma seemed to bear on her, triggering these overwhelming episodes.

With each panic attack, Jane's senses seemed to heighten, every sensation becoming magnified and intensified. The touch of her racing heartbeat, pounding against her chest, was a tangible reminder of the fear and anxiety coursing through her veins.

The sensation of her palms becoming damp and clammy, the moisture clinging to her skin, added to the discomfort, as if her body was physically manifesting the internal confusion she was experiencing.

The air she breathed felt heavy and suffocating, each breath becoming shallow and constricted. The smell of her fear, a distinct mix of adrenaline and unease, filled her nostrils, further exacerbating the sense of suffocation. It was as if the atmosphere around her was tainted with the scent of anxiety, intensifying her panic.

Accompanied by the shallow breaths, her frantic gasps vibrated in her ears. The world around her seemed to fade into the background as her focus narrowed, consumed by the overwhelming sound of her distress. It was a haunting symphony of panic, drowning out any other external noise.

They struck without warning, leaving her feeling vulnerable and helpless. The touch, smell, and sound of these episodes became intimately linked to the disorder that plagued her mind, a constant reminder of the fragility of her mental state.

These panic attacks birthed new monsters within Jane's psyche, giving rise to agoraphobia, a fear of open spaces, and paranoia, a constant companion of mistrust. These complex challenges cast long and dark shadows over her life, inflicting mental suffering that took an immense toll.

They robbed her of educational opportunities, held her back from potential career advancements, and made the most straightforward social interactions an uphill battle.

When Jane and John crossed paths during their first year of high school, she found an unexpected anchor in his presence. John became her pendulum of stability amid the turbulent sea of adolescence. With each encounter, his magnetic charm and genuine kindness cast a soothing spell on Jane's restless soul.

His mere presence brought a sense of reassurance and comfort like a wisp guiding her through the uncertainties of teenage life. Little did she know that their connection would deepen, shaping the course of their shared journey in ways neither of them could have foreseen.

John embodied the essence of adventure and unpredictability. His ruggedly handsome features, complete with tousled hair and a hint of stubble that bordered on a full beard, exuded a magnetic appeal. His broad shoulders and muscular physique further reinforced this image, creating an initial impression of unapproachability.

Yet, beneath his tough exterior lay a man of unparalleled sensitivity and compassion. His warm hazel eyes held a deep reservoir of empathy and kindness, revealing his true essence to those fortunate to see beyond his intimidating facade.

John possessed a depth of emotion that defied his rugged exterior, a tenderness that flowed through his veins and resonated in every interaction with his beloved wife, Jane.

Their love, solid and unwavering, ran deep within John's heart. Despite his adventurous spirit and sharp exterior, his affection for Jane knew no bounds, encompassing a deep tenderness that defied explanation. She was the beating pulse within his chest, the reason for his existence.

However, John's puzzling disappearance and his work's secrecy cast a blanket of doubt and uncertainty over their once unbreakable bond. Questions loomed, creating a gap of emotional distance that threatened to swallow their love whole.

Though marked by trials and tribulations, their shared journey forged a connection that surpassed bloodlines and familial ties.

In many ways, John mirrored Jane's father, not only in his devastatingly good looks but also in his analytical mind. From the first moment they met, Jane knew, with unwavering certainty, that he was destined to hold her heart.

Their relationship, a battlefield of its own, strained under the weight of Jane's internal struggles, rendering her unable to articulate the emotions swirling within her. The journey with John became jumbled, where understanding and connection seemed elusive.

# 2

The weight of Jane's last conversation with John continued to haunt her, lingering in her mind like an unwelcome melody that played on a never-ending loop. Its echoes resounded within her, day in and day out, as if the words spoken were etched into her soul.

*"Come on, Jane, I'm going to miss my flight," John said sternly. Jane hopped into the driver seat of the car and started the engine, and pulled out of the driveway,*

*"So, do you think you'll be gracing our Thanksgiving table this year?" Jane asked, her voice carrying a note of hopeful anticipation.*

*"I'm not certain, love," John replied, his tone heavy with regret. "Work is a frenzy right now, threatening more time than anticipated."*

*Jane's shoulders slumped in disappointment, a weary sigh escaping her lips. "I'm getting tired of crafting excuses for my sister, trying to explain why my husband is noticeably absent from every holiday celebration."*

*"Honey, it's not my intention to disappoint you. I'm juggling the demands of my job and our marriage as best as possible. You know how important this job is to me and its significant impact on our lives."*

*"But how can we label this a marriage when you're so evasive about your whereabouts and activities? It's downright not fair to me. Sometimes, I can't help but wonder if you're with that tramp you work with," Jane snapped, her voice bitter.*

*John's response was immediate, his tone a combination of disbelief and anger. "That's preposterous!" he exclaimed, his eyebrows knitting together in a frown. "You know I maintain a* clear line between my professional and personal relationships. I was upfront with you about the incident at the annual Christmas party when she, under the influence of alcohol, attempted to kiss me. I left the party early to avoid being the subject of any untrue gossip before I could clarify the situation. I was perhaps naive to think I was immune to such incidents, but when it happened, I dealt with it with due respect and transparency'"

Jane sat there in silence, tears rolling down her face, her mouth quivering as she spoke. "I wouldn't blame you," she began, her voice shaking. "I was forced to terminate our first pregnancy. I failed as a wife, as a mother, and as a human being. I knew how much you wanted kids, and I saw your face when the Doctor explained what happened. It felt like I was being read my last rites, and you said nothing. Weeks went by, and we never—."

John quickly interrupted, his voice rising and his face glistening with sweat. "I was in shock. My unborn child was gone, and my wife almost died, all within a few hours! I couldn't come to terms with it. Why did it have to happen? Who knows!"

*Jane was struggling to get her following words out. There was a look of emptiness that could not be filled, and all that remained was a heavy silence. Then, the silence was broken by the comforting touch of John's warm hand.*

*Each day, fragments of that conversation replayed in her mind, the words spoken becoming more vivid with each repetition. They danced like ghosts before her, their weight and significance growing heavier with each passing moment. It was a haunting refrain that refused to fade away, a song that seemed to have no end.*

*The touch of their last embrace, the sensation of his arms around her, lingered in her memory like a bittersweet caress. She could almost feel the warmth of his body, the gentle pressure of his fingertips against her skin, as if he was still there, holding her close. But with each replay, the touch became a phantom sensation, a reminder of what was lost and could never be again.*

*The sound of their voices, the inflections and tones that once filled the air with familiarity and love, now resonated as a painful reminder of their final exchange. Each word spoken haunted her,*

*their meaning and implications seeping into the depths of her*

*being.*

*Jane desired closure for a chance to rewrite the script of that*

*last conversation. She wished to mend the frayed ends, to find*

*relief in their final exchange. But the words remained frozen in*

*time, locked within the confines of her memory, replaying*

*relentlessly like a broken record.*


In the aftermath of John's sudden disappearance, Jane grappled

with a choppy sea of intense dreams, each carrying its weight. The

troubling sensation of survivor's guilt invaded her subconscious,

leaving her floating in the depths of her mind.

Jane's intricate narrative and the vivid landscapes of her dreams

escalated with every passing night. These nocturnal visions, rich

and detailed to the point of near lucidity, felt like realms beyond

her control, where she was a mere observer in her consciousness.

The conclusion of each dream marked an entropic transition into sleep paralysis, a state where her body refused to follow her commands to move, leaving her trapped in a perplexing stasis.

Yet, her senses remained acutely attuned to her surroundings, absorbing every minute detail with pristine clarity. This unsettling stillness became a gateway to her nightmares, unfolding before her like a grotesque theater, a gruesome performance she was powerless to escape.

Yet, among the confusion of her subconscious, Jane found peace in the routine tasks of her day-to-day life. It was during one such moment of normalcy that she discovered something peculiar. As she sifted through a packet of documents revealing Dash's lineage, her eyes were drawn to a few anomalies that seemed out of place.

"What's this scar doing on your neck, buddy?" she queried, addressing Dash, who responded with innocent, goofy eyes. "If I find out John had any hand in some shady dogfighting racket, I swear he wouldn't hear the end of it," she joked, injecting a touch of humor to offset the seriousness of her discovery.

With each passing day, the bond between Jane and Dash grows stronger, manifesting in their actions and interactions. Once filled with worry and uncertainty, Jane's voice transformed into a tender melody whenever she spoke to Dash. It conveyed adoration and care, resonating with their unspoken affection.

In the quiet moments they shared, Jane would sit beside Dash, their eyes meeting in a language only they understood. She would gently stroke his fur, feeling the warmth of his body against her hand as if their connection had transcended the physical realm. Dash, in turn, responded with a wag of his tail and a look of pure satisfaction, his eyes reflecting the trust and love he had for Jane.

Their bond was not limited to words or gestures alone. Jane would often surprise Dash with belly rubs, knowing it was one of his favorite indulgences. As her fingers traversed his soft belly, they communicated a language of comfort and companionship, a silent promise that she would always be there for him.

In return, Dash showered Jane with unwavering loyalty and a boundless affection that knew no bounds. Whether it was a gentle nudge of his nose against her hand or a playful lick on her cheek, he found ways to express his love and appreciation for the woman who had become his closest companion.

Their bond was verification of the power of unconditional love and the deep connection that can be forged between a human and a beloved animal. It was a bond that defied explanation, surpassing the limits of language and manifesting in the simple acts of love and care they shared.

Her voice mingled with the thumping of Dash's tail against the floor, a joyful tempo filling the room. "Who's a good boy?" she would coo, her words accompanied by the gentle caress of her hand through Dash's fur, a tactile display of affection.

Dash responded to this outpouring of love with enthusiastic licks, his wet tongue leaving a trail of slobbery kisses on Jane's face. The scent of his doggy breath, a familiar and comforting aroma, mingled with the sweet smell of the outdoors, reminding Jane of their adventures in the park.

During their strolls in the park, Dash became more than just a pet to Jane; he became the silent listener to her deepest thoughts and emotions.

The touch of Dash's fur beneath her fingers brought grounding as if his presence was a physical reminder that she was not alone. "You know, buddy, I miss him so much," she confided, her voice hinting nostalgia. Her fingers gently scratched behind Dash's ears, feeling the furry softness of his coat between her fingertips.

The touch of Dash's wet nose nuzzling against her cheek brought happiness as if his affection was a tangible embrace. "Who needs a man when you have a dog, right, buddy?" she quipped, laughter filling the room. Her laughter mingled with Dash's playful barks, creating an atmosphere of joy and companionship.

The touch of his paw against her leg provided a grounding presence, a reminder that she was safe in her home. The sound of Dash's gentle snores, a comforting lullaby, mingled with the distant hum of the night, providing a soothing soundtrack to her troubled mind.

In their quiet moments together, Jane was drawn to the details that made Dash unique. The touch of her fingers tracing the scar on his neck, with its uncanny resemblance to the letter 'J,' stirred a mix of emotions within her.

# 3

The scent of freshly brewed coffee filled the air, mingling with the faint aroma of Dash's fur. Dash became a source of support, a companion who offered his presence and affection without judgment or expectation. Each day unfolded for Jane in a shroud of uncertainty, a relentless question resonating in her mind –

*If he is dead, what was the cause of his death, and when had it occurred? Was it a swift, merciful ending, or was it drawn out, agonizing, reminiscent of the gruesome fatalities depicted in late-night horror flicks?*

The thought of his final moments was a hole she dared not gaze into. Merely contemplating, it brought hot, stinging tears to her eyes. 'John's death is all my fault. Or perhaps I'm already dead, and this is my personalized version of Hell.'

Jane lay on her bed, feeling as exposed and vulnerable as a raw wound. Her eyes were wet to the point of being sticky, the dried salt of her tears forming a crusty residue reminiscent of a bout of pink eye. Too drained to wipe it away, she surrendered to the beckoning arms of sleep.

As the night draped its inky veil over Jane's weary mind, a recurring dream trapped her in its unsettling grip. She navigated a barren highway in the ethereal realm, the solitude weighing heavy upon her soul. But instead of occupying the driver's seat, she was operating the vehicle from the back seat, a mere passenger in her subconscious theater.

Her eyes strained against the darkness, seeking comfort in the feeble glow of distant headlights. The steering wheel was behind the driver's seat, an inaccessible artifact denying her control over her trajectory. A troubling sensation of helplessness gnawed at her core with each passing moment.

Through the limited expanse of her obscured vision, she caught a glimpse of a car ahead, its presence a haunting silhouette against the dimly lit road. Her heart quickened, a surge of urgency flooding her veins. But as her foot instinctively reached for the brake pedal, her searching foot found only emptiness. The realization struck her cruelly - she was powerless to avert the impending collision.

Metal scraped against metal, a symphony of destruction that drowned out the rhythm of her racing heartbeat. The world spun in disarray, a whirlwind of chaos and despair.

As the echoes of the collision subsided, a sinister hush descended upon the scene. The wailing of distant sirens pierced the air, their mournful cries foreshadowing the arrival of law enforcement. Jane's heart pounded in her chest, a harsh rhythm that mirrored the turmoil churning within her.

Her trembling hands were bound by cold, unyielding handcuffs, the weight of guilt and fear settling upon her like a suffocating shroud. With a mixture of dread and disbelief, she watched as the medical team rushed to the aid of an unknown figure lying motionless on the ground.

Time slowed to a desolate crawl, each passing second etched with haunting clarity. The futile efforts of the medical professionals unfolded before her eyes, their desperate attempts to revive a life slipping away. The sounds of urgent commands and the distant wails of sirens mingled with the deafening silence surrounding her soul.

In the depths of her subconscious, a chilling truth beckoned - a fact that whispered of fault, remorse, and an irreversible chain of events forever etched in her memory. The dream, a twisted theater of her fears and regrets, lingered like a ghostly apparition, leaving her trembling in its wake.

Waking up the following day was like peeling an eggshell from her sensitive eyes. Dash was the first to rise, signaling the start of their morning routine.

Dash's stubbornness was an exasperating trait that frequently tested Jane's patience. Yet, the dog exhibited some peculiar habits that were not typical for puppies. Ordinarily, puppies would relieve themselves arbitrarily until proper training was enforced.

All she could manage was to let Dash out each morning, silently praying he'd do his business outside. Strangely, Dash did not soil the carpet, relieving himself on smoother surfaces such as in the bathroom or kitchen.

Each time Dash refrained from soiling the rug, Jane's mind was pulled back to memories of her husband. She remembered how she scolded him for tracking mud onto the carpet after his long trips.

He would be away for weeks, even months, and upon his return, the first thing he'd hear would be Jane's complaints about the state of the carpet. She could still see the guilty look in his eyes whenever he dirtied the rug upon his return.

As Jane navigated the complexity of a new puppy owner, she faced yet another source of concern. The dawn of Dash's first veterinary visit was imminent. A gnawing sense of anxiety was steadily building within her, twisting and turning like a serpent in the depths of her stomach.

Her bond with Dash had developed almost against her will, making the thought of potential loss a burden too heavy for her heart to bear. "What if he's sick? What if he has cancer? I can't bear to lose another loved one," she murmured.

Gathering her courage, Jane reached out to set her alarm clock for the early hour of 6:30 am before reducing the room into a sea of darkness with one swift motion of the light switch.

When dawn broke, Dash demonstrated an unusual reluctance to venture outside, leading to an untimely mess on the kitchen floor. With a sigh, Jane retrieved a towel from the laundry basket, forcing herself to clean it up.

As she scrubbed at the stains, her gaze drifted out of the window, catching sight of the sunset reflecting off the snow. She desired John's presence, to share the simple beauty of the moment with her.

As the clock's hands moved past the seventh hour, Jane readied herself for the day, putting on her coat and gathering her keys. With Dash's leash looped around her wrist, providing a sense of security and control, she noticed Dash's hesitation toward the snow.

Looking down at his nervous expression, she offered words of reassurance. "It's just some harmless snow, nothing to be afraid of." With those words, she fortified herself, ready to face the daunting uncertainty of Dash's first veterinary visit.

Navigating their path towards the passenger side of her SUV, Jane exerted every ounce of her strength to hoist Dash into the roomy center. The considerable effort nearly resulted in a pulled muscle, leaving her slightly irritated. "Seriously, why did I have to get the biggest dog breed?" she vented, her words peppered with exasperation.

As she maneuvered the SUV out of the driveway, her gaze inadvertently drifted toward her husband's car, now a silent relic of his existence.

Jane continued her journey along the pulsating artery of the road ahead. The hum of passing cars served as the background score to her mental replay of that last conversation with John.

Her daydream was abruptly shattered when she narrowly avoided colliding with the compact car ahead of her. In a rare reversal of roles, the road rage was not hers but stemmed from the other vehicle's driver.

Through her windshield, Jane caught sight of a figure glaring at her via the rear-view mirror of the car ahead. The car's back window was tinted so highly that it was impossible to distinguish the person's features or gender. Nevertheless, Jane was sure that if she could have seen the person, a glare would have been waiting for her.

After a moment, she detected a flurry of motion within the shadowy confines of the car. The faint outline suggested flailing arms, seemingly an expression of anger. Jane faked indifference, pretending to look away as if oblivious to the near-miss incident.

She averted her gaze no sooner than a powerful wave of déjà vu washed over her. The scene unfolding before her was eerily reminiscent of one of her recent dreams. Except in the dream, she had rear-ended the vehicle at a breakneck speed, leading to a subsequent scene of her being detained at a police station for vehicular homicide.

The road, the scenery, and the make and color of the car matched her dream with uncanny precision. Jane was left with the unsettling realization that her subconscious mind, armed with the memory of her vision, had prompted her to apply the brakes just in time, thereby averting a potentially devastating accident.

Jane was no stranger to sporadic episodes of clairvoyance, those short-lived moments where she seemed to perceive events beyond the natural senses. Although these instances had occurred a few times, this latest episode was the most overwhelming.

As the traffic flow resumed its normal rhythm, she maneuvered past the car involved in the near-miss incident, consciously avoiding eye contact with its driver. Jane could sense the driver's attempt to draw her attention, and she silently prayed that the individual was not some unhinged lunatic. A thought floated to her: 'You're still alive because of me.'

Eventually, Jane and Dash reached their destination - the vet's office. They were nearly half an hour early, but Jane stepped inside with hopeful anticipation, silently wishing that the vet would accommodate them ahead of schedule.

Despite the lack of pressing responsibilities, Jane always sought the most efficient way to navigate everyday situations. This instinctive tendency emphasized the human mind's intricate workings and calculating nature.

However, Jane reminded herself that conformity to collective norms should not be the sole driving force behind one's actions. After all, life was about more than just ticking clocks and adhering to expected timelines; it was about embracing the journey and the invaluable lessons it instructed.

# 4

Dash and Jane found themselves nestled in the cozy corner of a well-lit sitting area, draped with a warm ambiance of familiarity. Tracing the worn edges of an old magazine, Jane glanced at Dash.

His eyes, an auburn mosaic of despair and resignation, reflected the silent understanding of their reason for being there. It was as if he was embracing the temper tantrum of a defiant toddler, making guilt slither into Jane's heart.

Yet, she was determined, aware of the impending danger of a rabid dog or a fatal canine disease lurking in the shadows. She was ready to wield the cloak of responsibility, unwilling to postpone the inevitable.

"It's going to be okay; I promise!" she reassured Dash, her voice a comforting blanket in the sterile environment.

"Dash?" said the receptionist, her voice cutting through the heavy silence.

"Well, looks like it's your turn, dude," Jane spoke to Dash, almost as if expecting an understanding nod.

They rose from their seats, "Right this way, please," the receptionist guided them, her voice a gentle lullaby in the sterile ambiance. She was a young woman, perhaps in her mid-twenties, with flowing blonde locks, a slim figure, and a warm smile. As Jane looked at her, she couldn't help but let her mind wander to the receptionist's personal life, imagining intimate encounters and different lovers.

Jane was caught off guard by her feelings for this woman, a stranger, until that very moment. "Could I be attracted to her?" Jane questioned herself, wrestling with the newfound idea of homosexuality, previously unexplored in her heterosexual world. These feelings sparked a sense of curiosity within her. "What does this mean? Why now?" she wondered, feeling compelled to understand this surprising shift in her perceptions.

"The vet will be right with you," giving Jane a glance and a forced smile.

They were nestled in a compact room devoid of windows, the only light source being the harsh fluorescent bulbs overhead. The antiseptic odor of rubbing alcohol hung heavy in the air, intermingling with the overpowering scent of an older woman's pungent perfume.

The walls were a collage of posters featuring dogs of different breeds alongside many advertisements. These ranged from warnings about rabies and Parvo to information about fleas, ticks, and obscure diseases that Jane wasn't familiar with.

Intermittently, there were ads for local businesses, their signs screaming for attention, presumably unable to afford the luxury of a daytime TV commercial slot. Jane was already anticipating the hefty fee for the doctor's brief visit and feeling overwhelmed by the countless unrelated ads.

Dash started to show a deep sense of anxiety. Jane wished she could offer him some form of comfort, some reassurance in this sea of unfamiliarity.

After several minutes, the doctor emerged into the glaringly bright room. Compared to the stereotypical image of a male vet, he was in his early thirties, with a deep, bronzed complexion. His chiseled jawline framed a face adorned with dark, wavy hair, the texture of which Jane couldn't discern whether it was tamed with mousse or pomade.

A peculiar scar traced its path from the right side of his lip, disappearing halfway up his right nostril. His smile held an air of confidence, bordering on arrogance, reminiscent of someone who might have just paraded a brand-new Ferrari through a middle-class suburban neighborhood. As Jane studied him, she couldn't shake off the thought that he and the receptionist were possibly more than just professional acquaintances.

"How are we faring today?" he interjected, his tone mixed with a hint of playful sarcasm, effectively nudging Jane out of her trance.

"Pretty good, thank you," Jane responded, her voice barely audible in the pure silence. She averted her gaze, her cheeks flushing a soft shade of pink.

"I'm Doctor Argow." He extended a hand in an awkward greeting toward Jane.

"Nice to meet you; I'm Jane." She gestured towards Dash, her companion in this unfamiliar territory. "And this little guy is Dash. But you already know that, of course." Her voice wavered slightly, betraying her unease.

"It's great to meet you both." His voice held a comforting warmth, his smile inviting and kind. "Just a routine checkup today? Standard vaccinations and a health assessment?" Jane was momentarily lost, her mind scrambling to recall the reason for their visit. A gentle nudge from Dash's paw against her leg brought her back to the present.

"Of course! We're here for the vaccines and to ensure my little guy is healthy." Jane's voice held a playful undertone, her lips curling into a sly smirk and a teasing half-smile.

Despite the fear of making a manifestation of herself, she couldn't help but be swept away by a wave of nostalgia reminiscent of her carefree teenage years. As their interaction unfolded, Jane could feel her heart pounding against her ribcage, a knot of anxious anticipation tightening in her chest.

Her fingers tingled with a strange sensation as she fought to maintain her facade of calm composure. *Not right now. Please. Calm yourself, Jane.* Her breathing increased as she fought off the sudden panic attack.

Dr. Argow's laughter echoed in the room as he enlisted Jane's help to lift Dash onto the examination table. She responded with a bashful smirk, their combined efforts completing the task.

As he meticulously examined Dash's lush coat, he broadly grinned, complimenting, "No fleas or any other infestations, and his ears are as clean as a whistle. You must be doing an outstanding job grooming him."

His eyes landed on a scar etched on Dash's face. With a playful glint, he remarked, "I can't even begin to imagine the unbelievable task of bathing this behemoth!"

Jane's retort was quick with wit, "That's quite funny, considering your initial comment about possible infestations made it sound like we were living in filth."

She strained to maintain her composed demeanor, but the dryness in her mouth and the frantic pounding in her head hinted at the simmering panic within.

"All right, I'll be back momentarily with my thermometer and the first set of vaccines," he announced, his gaze locked with Jane's before he turned on his heel and exited the room, leaving Jane alone with her thoughts.

To distract herself, she began counting the seconds, each tick ringing in the quiet room. Her gaze drifted around the room, seeking a distraction, and landed on an advertisement on the wall.

The ad showcased a campaign soliciting donations for canine anatomy and DNA research to enhance pet health and safety. As her eyes traced the colorful visuals of the ad, a figure in the backdrop caught her attention. A man appeared to be bending over to pick up something. She squinted, her mind struggling to make sense of the blurry image. Recognition dawned on her, and her heart pounded in her chest.

The man in the picture bore an uncanny resemblance to her husband. She felt a surge of emotion welling within her, her eyes brimming with unshed tears. She was so absorbed in her discovery that she barely blinked. Her gaze fixed on the hauntingly familiar figure in the ad.

Suddenly, the door swung open, the abrupt noise shaking Jane out of her contemplation. She nearly leaped off her chair, her heart pounding in her chest, her mind a whirlwind of thoughts and emotions.

"Are you quite all right, miss?" Dr. Argow's voice held a hint of playful curiosity, his eyes sparkling with muted amusement. "My apologies if my entrance startled you."

Jane managed a small smile and whispered, "I'm all right. I was just lost in my thoughts when the door startled me."

Dr. Argow's gaze bore into Jane, his eyes narrowing as he studied her face discerningly. "You appear rather pale. Allow me to fetch you a Powerade from the break room." He swiftly exited the room, only to return moments later clutching a chilled, blue Powerade.

As Jane eagerly gulped down the drink, Dr. Argow watched in barely concealed surprise. After a moment, he asked, "Is everything okay?"

His voice held a trace of concern. Jane responded with a nod. Her eyes were still wide as she twisted the cap back onto the now-empty bottle. She cast a glance around the room in search of a trash bin.

Finding none, she carefully placed the empty bottle between her legs. She awaited Dr. Argow's next move with Dash, her attention still partly anchored on the unsettling image she had discovered moments ago.

Dr. Argow gently asked Jane to secure Dash while he prepared to take the dog's rectal temperature. "Okay, Dash, this might feel a bit chilly," he warned, his gaze meticulously trained on where the thermometer would be inserted.

He applied a generous layer of lubrication on the thermometer, the cold gel enhancing the clinical feel of the instrument. With a steady hand, he carefully guided the rigid shaft of the thermometer into Dash's rectum.

No sooner had the thermometer been inserted than Dash jerked in response, his whimper piercing the pure silence like a deep slumber abruptly shattered. Dr. Argow swiftly withdrew the thermometer, his brows furrowing in confusion.

The section of the thermometer that had been inserted was missing. A wave of bewilderment washed over his face, his eyes reflecting his surprise. He remained motionless for a few heartbeats, his mind racing to make sense of the unexpected turn of events. After a few moments, he finally broke the uncomfortable silence, lifting his head to face Jane, his face a mask of measured calm.

"Hmm, perhaps the decision to switch thermometer brands wasn't our best move," he chuckled lightly, his lips curling into a kind smirk. As he spoke, Jane noticed a subtle thinning of hair at the crown of his head, the onset of a receding hairline making a shy debut. Like the condensation on the outer surface of a chilled shot glass, beads of sweat began forming on his forehead, proof of his rising nerves.

"We recently transitioned to a new equipment provider as a cost-saving measure," he explained, shaking his head slightly. "It appears the thermometer snapped during Dash's brief moment of panic. However, there's no cause for alarm. The broken piece should naturally exit his system during his next bowel movement." His words were laced with reassurance, his smile attempting to diffuse the tension.

"Only a tiny fragment, barely an inch, broke off. And incidentally, these thermometers are mercury-free," Dr. Argow added, a hint of pride creeping into his voice as he sought to downplay the unusual incident.

"I'd be more than willing to retrieve it," Dr. Argow proposed, his voice mixed with a physical sense of relief, a faint smirk on his lips. "However, we've already seen how Dash responds to foreign objects in his anus."

His gaze fell on the discarded thermometer, his eyes widening as he noted the reading. It displayed an alarming 120 degrees Fahrenheit, and the numbers were still climbing.

"It seems we're dealing with a defective device here," he muttered, his tone shifting to a more professional manner. "I must inform our tech team to explore other brands." His eyes returned to Dash, his gaze appraising.

"Fortunately for us, Dash appears to be in excellent health for a dog of his age and breed," he concluded confidently.

Clearing his throat, he leaned closer to Jane and muttered, "Tough crowd," his voice barely whispered, uncertain if she had caught his words.

Jane appeared to be listening, her gaze wandering around the room. But her mind was elsewhere, operating on autopilot, her hand absently stroking Dash's head in a comforting rhythm.

Sensing what was next, she braced herself as Dr. Argow's voice filled the room, his tone soothing yet firm, "We're going to proceed with his first round of vaccinations now. He'll likely be drowsy over the next day and might not eat much. Adverse reactions are rare but do occur, so it'll be important to keep a close eye on him for the next few hours."

His gaze shifted back to the discarded thermometer, his voice carrying a note of resolve, "This incident serves as a potent reminder for us all to research our equipment choices thoroughly— and never to compromise on quality."

Half-absorbed, Jane responded casually, "It's fine; I can stay with him until he feels better." Dr. Argow brought out a syringe, filling it with a transparent liquid before moving toward Dash. Jane's grip on Dash tightened, her instincts on high alert to prevent further complications.

As the needle pressed against Dash's skin, Jane caught a fleeting glimpse of the Doctor's face from her peripheral vision. The sudden change in his expression was enough to signal that something was amiss.

"What use is a needle that can't penetrate the skin?" Dr. Argow mused aloud, his tone laced with frustration. "Perhaps it could double as a poor excuse for a squirt gun or serve as some sort of practical joke," he added, forcing a half-smile onto his face, his mind grappling with the situation's absurdity.

"Ha-ha, very funny," Jane interjected, her voice dry. His efforts to administer the injection intensified, his teeth grinding in concentration until the needle unexpectedly bent at a sharp right angle. "Um, I'm guessing that's not supposed to happen?"

"No, it certainly isn't," Dr. Argow admitted, his voice tinged with irritation. "It's almost as if these needles are made of aluminum. Perhaps my technician took my cost-cutting instruction a bit too literally. Sometimes, if you want something done right, you have to do it yourself," he grumbled, his expression deceiving his annoyance.

With a resigned sigh, Dr. Argow rose from his chair, informing Jane that they would need to reschedule their appointment once his new supplies arrived. He was profuse in his apologies.

"Small pups like Dash are particularly susceptible to certain diseases, but these can be effectively prevented with vigilant care," he mentioned with a wry smile. "Ensure that he sticks to his regular diet and drinks ample water. Don't hesitate to bring him in if you observe any unusual behavior. I assure you, on your next visit, we'll get things done right." He raised his eyebrows for emphasis, his tone earnest. "And, of course, there will be no charge for today's visit. I sincerely apologize for the inconvenience."

"Well, thanks for trying," Jane said, standing up and clipping Dash's leash back onto his collar. The receptionist tried to say goodbye, but Jane ignored her and pretended to check her shirt for a nonexistent stain.

As she drove away, she noticed the receptionist and Dr. Argow talking near the window, and he seemed to be staring at her a few times. Feeling a bit awkward, Jane waved quickly before driving off.

"Was everything okay, Doctor?" The receptionist's voice held a note of concern as she addressed Dr. Argow.

"Y... Yes," he stammered, a blush creeping onto his face. "I'm rather embarrassed about her initial experience here," he confessed, his voice barely above a whisper.

"But that was her, correct?" The receptionist pressed on, her curiosity piqued.

"Yes, that was indeed her," he confirmed, his eyes avoiding her probing gaze.

"I wish you'd explain why her visit was so significant," her tone laced with curiosity.

"All you need to understand is that she must remain a client," Dr. Argow responded rudely, his tone final.

"Uh, okay, weirdo. Why so serious?" The receptionist's question hung in the air, her teasing tone failing to mask her confusion.

"Let's just drop the subject," Dr. Argow suggested, his patience wearing thin.

"But," - the receptionist began, only to be swiftly interrupted by Dr. Argow's sudden outburst.

"Enough! I said drop it, damn it!" His voice echoed in the room. With a swift turn, he stormed off, the sound of a door slamming resonating in the now-silent room.

The receptionist stood rooted to her spot, a picture of befuddlement. She struggled to process the unexpected temper from Dr. Argow, a blatant disparity to his usual demeanor.

Shaking her head in a futile attempt to dispel the confusion enveloping her mind, she was left with a string of unanswered questions. She found herself drawn into the paradox of Jane, wondering what made her so unique in the Doctor's eyes.

On the other side of town, Jane was driving back home, her mind a whirlwind of thoughts about the day's events at the clinic. The awkwardness of her first visit was still fresh in her memory, but she was resolute to see the process through. Dr. Argow's assistance was greatly appreciated, yet something about him stirred a sense of unease within her.

She saw a familiar vehicle parked nearby as she turned into her driveway. Although this was the same car as before, something triggered in her subconscious that overpowered her reality.

It was John's car. Her heartbeat quickened, an unexpected flutter of anticipation coursing through her veins at the realization that he had returned. She parked her car and began her walk towards the front door, her emotions churning within her.

As she swung open the door, she was greeted by the sight of John. He was seated on the couch, his face a melancholy portrait as he looked up at her.

# 5

John, a hint of remorse seemingly carved into his facial features, rose from the worn-out armchair, his movements slow and hesitant. "Jane, my sincerest apologies," he began, his voice thick with guilt and regret, as if acknowledging a mistake. He strolled towards her, each step a testimony to his sincere plea. "I fully acknowledge my mistake and want to repair it."

She observed him, her eyes overflowing with tears, but she chose to cloak her thoughts in silence, knowing deep down that he wasn't truly there. John pivoted on his heel, his heart heavy in his chest, and approached the door. But as he reached for the knob, a whisper halted him. "Wait," Jane urged, her voice frail but insistent, desperately clinging to the illusion she had created. "Stay."

Surprised, John swiveled around, his eyes wide as saucers. Gathering her courage, Jane approached him and wrapped her arms around him in a tight embrace. Their tears mingled, each drop a testament to their pain and longing, as they held onto each other like lifelines in a storm. It was a moment of reconciliation that rekindled their belief in their love—a love worth every battle.

Jane brushed away her tears as they gradually disentangled, giving John a hopeful smile. "I forgive you," she declared, her words lifting a burdensome weight from her shoulders. John reciprocated her smile, a wave of relief washing over him like a refreshing summer rain.

"I love you," he breathed, gently pressing his lips against hers. A sweet interlude made Jane sense a slice of happiness and peace for the first time in weeks.

She knew they still had mountains to climb and storms to weather, but she also knew they were stronger together. Jane allowed herself to dream of a future where everything would be okay. Side by side on the couch, immersed in a conversation about their future, Jane and John started mending their fractured relationship stitch by stitch.

With a jolt, Jane's eyelids fluttered open, her gaze meeting the harsh reality of an empty room. The vividness of her daydream had tricked her senses into believing John was there, his absence hitting her with startling clarity. It was a figment of her imagination, a desperate plea woven from the threads of longing for a reality that didn't exist.

She exhaled heavily, an audible demonstration of her isolation. She yearned for his presence, the comfort and familiarity that John had once brought into her life. But she also knew she couldn't keep grasping onto the fleeting wisps of their past. She had to let go to free herself from the chains of yesteryears and step forward into the unmapped landscape of her future.

Yet, with the departure of John from her world, Jane's mind had begun to paint illusions of his presence. In the silent theater of her dreams, she would glimpse his face, feel the ghost of his touch feather-light against her skin, and hear whispered echoes of his voice, as soothing as a lullaby.

It felt as though John was still tethered to her, his spirit refusing to leave her side even in death. She understood the unhealthy nature of her hallucinations but found herself powerless to resist.

Shaking off her negative thoughts, Jane wandered into the kitchen, her heart burdened by sadness. As she methodically chopped a medley of vegetables and set a pot of pasta to boiling, her mind drifted to the peculiar encounter at the veterinary clinic earlier that day. Dr. Argow's erratic behavior had set off alarm bells in her mind, and she couldn't entirely dispel the nagging sense of unease.

Her train of thought was abruptly interrupted by the shrill ring of her phone. The screen displayed an unknown number. Blinking away her surprise, she picked up the call, her curiosity piqued. "Hello?" she said, trying to keep her voice steady.

"Hello, Jane. This is Dr. Argow," the voice on the other end of the line murmured, its familiarity sending a chill down her spine.

"Oh, hi," Jane responded, her voice blending relief and apprehension. The call was unexpected, and she wasn't sure what to make of it. It was not an appropriate amount of time for a follow-up call.

"I just thought I'd inquire about Dash's health," Dr. Argow continued, his voice eerily calm, like the still surface of a deep, dark pond.

"He's doing okay," Jane replied, grateful for the change in topic. "Thanks for asking."

"That's good to hear," Dr. Argow said, a hint of satisfaction creeping into his voice. "I realize our initial encounter was... uncomfortable. I wanted to extend my apologies and propose a fresh start. Together, we can ensure Dash receives the care he requires."

A shard of guilt hit Jane. She had quickly judged Dr. Argow based on his somewhat peculiar demeanor. Still, his apparent concern for Dash suggested a different side to him. Perhaps she needed to be corrected in her initial assessment.

"I appreciate that," Jane admitted, her voice softening slightly. "And I apologize for my attitude earlier. It's just been a difficult couple of weeks."

"I completely understand," Dr. Argow said, his voice oozing sympathy. There was something about the way he said it that was just a touch too eager, a tad too insincere. "Remember, don't hesitate to call if you need anything."

"Thanks, I'll keep that in mind," Jane responded, a tremor running down her spine as she ended the call, the unease from their encounter at the clinic resurfacing.

Jane found herself cradling a faint spark of hope as the call ended. Perhaps the tide was finally turning. Navigating back into the kitchen, she completed preparing her dinner and settled down to eat.

A wave of calmness washed over her, an unfamiliar yet welcome sensation. She knew the hurdles ahead but recognized the strength reservoir within herself. For the first time in what felt like forever, she believed everything would eventually return to normal.

Finishing her meal, Jane realized that her pantry was nearing empty. Seeing this as an opportunity to clear her mind with a drive, she decided to venture out to the grocery store alone. As she approached her car, a brightly colored flyer flapping on her windshield caught her eye.

It was advertising a pet adoption event at the local park. A smile graced her lips as she realized how long it had been since she'd been in the company of other animals. The adoption event could be a chance to find a buddy for Dash.

Fueled by this impulse, Jane set off toward the park, her heart fluttering with anticipation at the thought of various animals awaiting her. But as she pulled up, her heart skipped a beat. An unsettling figure was lurking in the shadows—Dr. Argow. But a second glance revealed nothing more than the soft shadows cast by the trees.

Drawing it up to her imagination, Jane stepped out of her car. She began to move toward the adoption event. However, an eerie feeling of being watched clung to her like a second layer of skin. She whirled around, her gaze scanning the expanse of the park, but found nothing out of the ordinary.

A sudden chill slithered down her spine as a phantom touch brushed her shoulder. She spun around, only to be met by an empty park.

The silence seemed to press in around her, and the once comforting shadows now seemed menacing. Her heart pounded like a wild drum as she hurried back to her car, the unsettling events casting a gloomy shadow over her once hopeful mood.

A sinister sense of unease stuck to her as Jane navigated the familiar roads back home. What was developing within her? Was she peering in the face of insanity? She desperately attempted to rationalize her experiences, attributing them to fatigue or stress. But a troubling suspicion deep within her subconscious refused to be silenced—something was undoubtedly amiss.

Upon reaching home, she secured all the doors and windows. The mundane act of locking up heightened her sense of security. As she settled onto her couch, attempting to persuade her frayed nerves into submission, a sudden knock at the door sent her heart catapulting into her throat.

Could it be Dr. Argow? She tiptoed to the door, gazing through the peephole, only to find an empty porch.

Her sigh of relief resonated through the silent house, yet the residual tension refused to dispel. Deciding to call it a night, she retreated to her bed, praying sleep would usher in a new, more peaceful day.

As dawn broke, Jane awoke feeling somewhat rejuvenated. She attributed the previous day's events to exhaustion and stress, hoping to dismiss them as mere figments of her overactive imagination. As she began her morning routine, she noticed a flyer on her kitchen table—the same one from her windshield. Picking it up, she was swept up in a wave of Deja vu.

A knock at the door shattered her daydream, her heart
pounding. She cautiously approached the door, peering through the
peephole. Yet again, no one was there. She brushed it off,
determined to believe it was a figment of her imagination.

As the day unfolded, however, the residual unease from the
previous day clung to her tightly. Despite her best efforts, the
sensation of being observed trailed her like a mirrored
doppelgänger. Seeking support, Jane and Dash strolled into the
park, hoping the crisp air and greenery would clear her mind.

But the momentary sensation of a cold touch on her shoulder
sent trembles of fear coursing through her. She spun around, her
heart hammering, but was met with nothing but the empty park.

A sickening realization dawned on her: this was not the product
of an overworked imagination. Struggling to control her irregular
breathing, she assured herself there had to be a rational
explanation.

Her eyes flicked from one corner of the park to the other,
desperately seeking the source of her torment. As she ventured into

a more secluded part of the park, the eeriy familiar cold touch returned, this time lingering against her skin like an icy whisper of dread. It was accompanied by a soft, uncanny story that seemed to curl around her ear, chilling her to the bone.

"You can't escape me, Jane."

Panic erupted within her like a volcano, obliterating any resemblance of rational thought. Her heart pounded against her ribs like a wild beast in a cage as she pivoted and broke into a frantic sprint. She couldn't decipher why these events were unfolding, but the need to find answers propelled her forward.

Upon reaching her house, she threw the door open and slammed it shut behind her. Her heart continued its relentless signal against her chest, a loud soundtrack to her escalating terror.

Summoning Dash to her side, Jane poured out her fears and experiences, her voice wavering between desperation and disbelief. She sought comfort in his presence, hoping to convince herself and Dash that she wasn't spiraling into madness. Dash, in response, stood panting by her side, his loyal eyes reflecting empathy and concern.

As night fell, Jane and Dash surrendered to the lull of sleep, their bodies nestled close in search of warmth and comfort. However, a chilling sensation creeping up her arm nudged Jane awake. Her heart pounded, fear prickling her skin as her eyes took in the ominous figure looming at the foot of her bed.

The room's shadows played 'hide and seek,' cloaking the figure's face. Yet, the sinister curvature of a grin was chillingly visible in the dim light.

Paralyzed by fear, Jane was trapped in her own body, an unwilling spectator to this terrifying vision. Each attempt to regain control, to force her body to react, only amplified her sense of helplessness.

"I told you, Jane... You can't escape me."

Her terrified scream shattered the silence, ricocheting off the walls. The figure dissipated in the blink of an eye, leaving a detectable residue of fear. Jane and Dash were left trembling, their hearts pounding in sync with the deafening silence that followed.

The urgency to act was undeniable, yet the path forward was uncertain. Whom could they trust with this terrifying truth? Who would help them navigate this nightmarish reality?

# 6

At the blush of dawn, Jane and Dash embraced the appeal of a clean slate. Determined to shake off the shackles of their monotonous existence, they ventured on a spontaneous voyage into the vast, leafy countryside.

Their vehicle cut a swift path through the morning air, as fresh as a mountain stream and peppered with the spicy scent of dew-kissed foliage. The wind, a spirited accomplice in their escape, ruffled their hair and caressed their faces while the sun, resplendent in its morning glory, draped them in a warm, golden embrace. The taste of freedom was rich and sweet, like the first bite of a ripe peach.

As they navigated the meandering country lanes, the soundtrack of their journey was an orchestra of nature's symphony - the harmonious chirping of the birds, the rustling whisper of leaves, and the rhythmic hum of the car's engine. Among this melody, Jane and Dash engaged in an animated discourse that, in its own unique way, blurred the lines between human speech and canine expression. The day was ripe with promise, and they were poised to pluck it.

"Isn't this a beautiful day for a drive, buddy?" Dash wagged his tail enthusiastically, his eyes bright with excitement.

"Woof! Woof!" Jane chuckled at Dash's response, knowing he shared her sentiment.

"You know, Dash, I've felt a bit reserved lately. But with you by my side, those barriers seem to disappear." Dash tilted his head and licked Jane's hand affectionately as if understanding her words.

"Ruff! Ruff!" Jane smiled, grateful for Dash's companionship and their unspoken understanding.

"It's amazing how you bring out the real me, Dash. I can be myself and be comfortable." Dash nuzzled against Jane's leg, his presence radiating comfort and acceptance.

"Arf! Arf!" Dash's tone increased in frequency as they exchanged nuances.

Jane's heart swelled with affection for her furry friend as they continued their journey, basking in the warmth of their unique connection.

Their trip led them to a charming little town, its quaintness inviting them to explore. Their stomachs led them to a small diner, its rustic charm reminiscent of a golden era. Jane enjoyed a hearty lunch of a juicy burger and crispy fries. Savoring each bite while Dash eagerly waited for bits and pieces to be shared by Jane.

Their eyes absorbed the hustle and bustle of the townsfolk, immersed in their routines—a scenic view of life's mundane yet delightful moments.

Their exploration continued post-lunch with a stroll around the town. A curiosity shop caught their eye—a treasure trove of antiquities. Inside, an old music box captivated Jane, its rustic charm compelling her to buy it on an impulsive whim.

Back on the road, Jane couldn't resist unveiling the music box as she lifted the delicate lid; a sweet melody filled the car, its soft notes dancing in the air, a soothing warmth against the day's frigid weather.

However, as the melody played, an unsettling atmosphere shift prickled Jane's senses. The once lovely tune warped into a sinister serenade, and a chilling sense of impending doom began to coil around her like a constrictor.

A glance at Dash revealed him happily oblivious to the change, his tail wagging in delight, amplifying the contrast between her growing fear and his innocent joy.

The ordinary music box, an artifact of forgotten times, seemed to radiate a spectral aura, suggesting its silent involvement in the mystery that had taken up residence in her life.

As Jane and Dash approached their home, the first rays of the sun were beginning to peek over the frost-kissed roof. The sun danced upon the snow-blanketed surface, transforming each flake into a dazzling diamond in a sea of brilliance.

She guided the car into the driveway, its tires crunching over the snow as she parked next to the familiar figure of her husband's vehicle. From the passenger seat, a soft whimper punctured the serene silence - Dash, with his round, soulful eyes brimming with anticipation, was ready to escape the confines of the car.

With a soft click, she unlatched the car door, and Dash sprang from the vehicle like a shot from a cannon. His paws pattered against the snow-dusted sidewalk as he trotted to the front door, his tail wagging. Dash darted in as she opened the door, making a beeline for his favorite spot beside the couch.

As darkness draped itself over the town, Jane, driven by determination, plunged into a web of the music box's history. She illuminated the room with the faint glow of her computer screen, her eyes scanning lines of text like a miner panning for gold.

She unearthed a yellowed newspaper clipping in the cobwebbed corner of the internet. It told a chilling tale of a woman named

Amelia, swallowed by time over a century ago, last seen cradling a music box identical to Jane's recent acquisition.

As Jane investigated more intensely, she was lured into the shadowy recesses of Amelia's tormented past, her obsession with the music box painted vividly across the archived pages.

An invisible thread seemed to knit Jane and Amelia together across the chasm of time. Could the spectral echoes of Amelia's life ring through the music box's haunting gambit? The possibility sent a shiver of anxiety down Jane's spine, but she couldn't ignore the magnetic pull of the mystery.

Late one evening, under the watchful gaze of Dash, she addressed the music box directly. "Amelia," she began cautiously, her voice barely more than a whisper in the silent room, "are you hidden within this melody? What message are you so desperate to convey?"

The spine-chilling tune swelled in the room, the temperature plummeting as if winter had claimed the space. An overwhelming presence swept through, dense as if a veil had been drawn between

Jane and the rest of the world, trapping her in an intense stroll with the image of Amelia's past.

"I'm here to assist you, Amelia," Jane whispered, her voice trembling in the cold air. "Guide me to what you need."

With Dash as her only anchor to reality, Jane stepped onto a crooked path, seeking the truth of Amelia's disappearance and the secrets within the music box.

She clung to the notion that the spirit of Amelia was leading her, nurturing a slender hope that this shadowy guide was a compassionate force propelling her toward the truth.

She was battling not only the invisible forces threatening her very existence but also endeavoring to grant Amelia's restless spirit the tranquility and closure it so desperately longed for.

The intensity of their endeavor magnified exponentially, nudging Jane dangerously close to the face of her sanity. The supernatural symphony of the music box wove itself into the fabric of her consciousness. It served as a chilling reminder, a metronome that kept time with her pulse, of the determined journey she had undertaken and the threats that lurked in the shadows ahead.

Jane nestled beside Dash on the couch, the warmth encasing her like a cocoon. As she drifted into a peaceful slumber, her dreams were painted with a panorama of swirling colors, a kaleidoscope suspended within a haze of fluffy clouds. Like a vivid watercolor painting, the dreamscape filled her sleep with a relaxing serenity.

*In the strange tapestry of her dream, Jane observed John packing by their bed, his movements flowing like a symphony. As she entered the room, he spun around, a perplexing smile lighting up his face, his expression an ambiguous sonnet she desired to decipher. Drawn towards the bathroom, she began to attend to her tangled hair and makeup.*

*As she bent to retrieve her brush, her gaze was captured by the mirror's reflection. John's spectral figure hovered behind her, his form wavering as if stitched from the threads of the morning fog.*

*His features blurred and faded into a misty white canvas, his smile finally dissolving as the dream shifted gears.*

*Suddenly, she was enveloped by the claustrophobic darkness of a coal mine, the air heavy with the scent of damp earth and the ghostly echoes of forgotten labor. The familiarity of her surroundings had evaporated, replaced by a chilling sense of alienation. The dream presented her with a sign: a yellow canary, self-suspended by a fishing line, a warning in the depths of the mine.*

*John was occupied in a calm conversation with a stranger to his left. The person's distinctive features include a weather-beaten face, a thick mustache like a crow's wing, and shoulder-length, dirt-streaked blonde hair. Despite Jane's approach, they remained oblivious to her, their figures dusted in soot, their whispers like the rustling of dried leaves.*

*She strained to interpret their conversation, but before she could piece together the puzzle, the stranger passed a document to John, who swiftly concealed it in his side pocket. Then, like a moth drawn to a flame, he began to stride towards a distant, glowing*

*beacon. Suddenly, the mine was shattered by the loud screech of*

*an alarm, a flashing red light slashing through the inky depths.*

*A chilling premonition gripped Jane's heart, her intuition*

*screaming that something catastrophic was on the horizon.*

*Propelled by a surge of adrenaline, she sprinted after John,*

*plunging deeper into the darkness. Her body was slick with fear-*

*induced perspiration as she chased the dwindling light of John's*

*silhouette.*

The shrill cry of the telephone shattered the tranquility, its ring

sliced through the air like a blade. Yet, when Jane was seized from

the clutches of her dreams, the answering machine had already

picked up.

A metallic, automated voice, devoid of human warmth,

resonated throughout the room. "Please leave a message after the

tone."

"Hello Jane," a voice slithered from the machine, its tone

uncomfortably calm. It was Doctor Argow from the vet clinic.

Each syllable he pronounced seemed to linger in the air like an apparition refusing to fade away. "I must apologize again for the unfortunate incident ye-yesterday."

As he continued, a sense of unease crept into the room, wrapping itself around Jane like a cold shroud. "To make amends," he persisted, his voice oozing insincere politeness, "I would like to invite you out for dinner." His proposition hung in the air, a spider waiting in its web.

"Or," he added, the pause before the word stretching out like a predator ready to pounce, "if you'd prefer, I could order take-out and drop it off at your place." His words punctured the silence, each one resonating with an unsettling intimacy.

"It's the least I can do for wasting your time and nearly putting Dash in harm's way."

His request for a callback sounded more like a command, his tone veiling a sense of control beneath its surface courtesy. "Please," he urged, "call me back at the clinic when you can." It was a plea that echoed in the stillness of the room.

"Thank you, and I'm eagerly waiting to hear from you soon," he concluded, his farewell leaving a bitter aftertaste. "Goodbye," he said, his voice fading into the emptiness, leaving a chilling sense of unease behind.

Reviving from her nap, Jane blinked at the soft afternoon light filtering through the window. Her eyes drifted to the clock, whose hands steadfastly pointed toward 4:30 pm.

She'd been asleep for far longer than she had planned. A sudden spark of concern shot through her heart as she noticed the apparent absence of Dash.

Compelled by intuition, she walked towards John's study, an entire room, almost sanctified since his departure. The door creaked open to reveal Dash perched by the window, his silhouette framed against the waning daylight. His eyes, wide and curious, were trained on the world outside.

With relief, she reached out and gently clasped his collar, her fingers brushing against the soft fur. She guided him out of the room, her heart heavy with memories and the desire to escape its melancholy atmosphere.

Retracing her steps, she again hit the play button on the answering machine. This time, she tuned into the faint tremor in Dr. Argow's voice, a nervousness masked by a coating of politeness. As the realization dawned on her, she couldn't help but feel a mix of surprise and suspicion - he was inviting her for a date.

She knew that healing would require time, a luxury she was willing to grant herself before contemplating a date. Despite this, the unexpected attention from Dr. Argow was like a soft ray of sunlight piercing the clouds, a mild flattery that warmed her heart.

Despite her reservations, she decided to accept his invitation. However, she made a mental note to tread carefully. She had no intention of being knotted in a romantic entanglement with the receptionist, nor did she want to stir a cauldron of unwanted drama. Her heart needed peace, not a love triangle's sharp and unpredictable edges.

How things had concluded with John was seared into her memory, leaving her heart delicate and vulnerable. The thought of entrusting it to another felt like crossing a high wire without a safety net. She was unsure if Dr. Argow could be a safe harbor for her heart and soul.

Simultaneously, she was mildly captivated by his receptionist, and the idea of exploring new romantic terrains flickered across her mind. But she immediately recognized that his attention was purely professional, a friendly facade to maintain a smooth business relationship and avert potential legal complications.

Her fingers curled around the corded phone, and the familiar dial tone hummed in her ear. But as she began to dial the vet clinic's number, she abruptly halted, slamming the receiver down with a resonating thud. The realization that the office would be closed at this hour washed over her. The decision, she concluded, could wait until tomorrow.

In the ensuing silence, Jane was confronted by her fears of being hurt again. It had been at least nine months since she had last ted the sweetness of intimacy; her last encounter had been a scheduled, passionless event borne more out of obligation than desire.

As the evening hours subsided away, Jane concealed herself on her couch, the flickering light from her trusty old television casting dancing shadows on her face. A faint smile graced her lips as she channel-surfed, eventually settling on her favorite home and gardening shows.

Jane was fascinated by the innovative design concepts and hands-on projects that shrouded her television screen. The notion of crafting something that was both aesthetically pleasing and practical with her own hands resonated deeply within her. It kindled a spark of purpose within her soul.

Jane had always been a woman who relished the satisfaction of a well-done DIY project. The sensation of the tools in her hand, the transformation of raw materials into something meaningful, had always been therapeutic.

Her focus was solely on her reconstruction journey, piecing her life back together one project at a time. It was a painstakingly slow process, but she was fueled by a tenacious spirit, a spark of determination that refused to be extinguished.

As the witching hour approached, Jane was wrestling with sleep, tossing and turning in the sea of her thoughts. Dash's breathing at the foot of the bed was a soothing lullaby, a gentle reminder of another living being sharing her space. Dr. Argow's words repeated in her mind's cinema, fueling her nocturnal contemplation. *How should she respond in the morning?*

It didn't have to be a romantic endeavor; it could simply be an enjoyable evening. But then, the question of Dash's care while she was out loomed large. Still in his puppyhood, Dash was a ball of energy waiting to unleash chaos at the slightest opportunity.

A solution struck her like a lightning bolt - her neighbor had once owned a St. Bernard who succumbed to kidney failure at a young age. Indeed, they would still have the cage she could borrow for Dash. With her mind at ease, she accepted Dr. Argow's offer.

As she mentally cataloged her tasks for the following day, she eventually fell asleep at 1:30 AM.

*Jane found herself immersed in the aroma of wildflowers, their scent intertwining with the salty tang of the sea. The symphony of waves crashing against the shore plays in the background, a soothing serenade by Mother Nature. Rising to her feet, she felt the sun's rays carpet her skin with a gentle warmth, contrasting the cool, yielding sand beneath her bare feet.*

*Her gaze was drawn to an anomaly on the otherwise pure shore - a dark, amorphous shape washed up by the waves. From a distance, it was a paradox; its identity was shrouded in mystery. With a curious heart, Jane approached the strange object, only to be met with a sight that stole her breath away.*

*A diminutive figure bearing an uncanny resemblance to Dr. Argow stood before her. The figure wore a vivid red jumpsuit and a white doctor's coat. His bare feet were sunk into the sand, an eyepatch lending him an air of intrigue. He was as still as a* sculpture, his silence and lack of movement adding to the surreal tableau.

"Hey! Can you hear me?" Jane called out, her voice swallowed by the expanse of the beach. The figure remained unmoving, his expression a frozen mask, causing a ripple of hesitation to wash over Jane before she reached out to touch him. He set off towards a distant black object on the shore, seemingly unaware of Jane's presence.

As they neared the object, Jane's heart clenched in shock. It was another man dressed in a black suit and tie solemnly. With surprising strength, Dr. Argow hoisted him onto his shoulder and began to walk away. It was John, his eyes open yet vacant. Her heart plummeted, a stone sinking in the ocean of her despair.

As she drew closer, John's head turned slowly in her direction. In an unsettling twist, he winked at her, a sinister half-smile playing on his lips. Before she could react, the two men vanished into thin air, leaving Jane alone on the beach.

*Suddenly, the tranquil beach morphed into a nightmare. The azure sea turned a sinister hue of red, each wave crashing onto the shore with violent fury, annihilating everything in its path and leaving a gruesome tide of thick, crimson blood in its wake. The once soft sand sprouted sharp spikes, piercing her feet with every step, while the lush grass transformed into a raging inferno. Consumed by the flames, she fell face-first into hell, the dream's horrifying climax jolting her awake.*

She awoke in a cold sweat as if she had leaped out of a steaming hot tub in the middle of a wintry evening. She managed to reign in her breathing before it spiraled out of control. She gently laid her head back down and squeezed out a single tear as she shut her eyes and drifted back to sleep.

*Awakening to her blood-curdling screams, Jane was trapped in the coils of another dreadful nightmare, the latest in a relentless series that had held her captive for weeks. Each dream was more visceral, more horrifying than the last, and they were accompanied by an unshakeable sensation of being observed by an evil entity.*

*This shadowy figure seemed intent on causing her harm.*

As the days morphed into an indistinguishable blur, Jane gradually descended into a chasm of paranoia and terror. She perceived spectral movements in her peripheral vision and heard sinister whispers punctuating the night's tranquility. The unsettling belief that she was being stalked and scrutinized latched onto her psyche, refusing to let go.

She sought professional help, but her pleas were brushed aside. The medical professionals prescribed a combination of drugs and therapy sessions. Yet, they were mere band-aids on a festering wound. Jane was trapped in her mind, tormented by her inner demons.

Eventually, Jane was swallowed whole by her insanity, an unfortunate casualty of her mind. Her once cherished DIY projects and home improvement shows were relegated to the forgotten corners of her past, commandeered by the sinister darkness that had seized her. She had become a tragic figure, a ghost lost within

her fears and self-doubts.

# 7

As the dawn celebrates a new day, Jane awakened from her slumber, her faithful canine companion Dash nestled close to her, his tail whipping the air in a frenzy of excitement. As she glanced out the window from her warm, familiar kitchen, a sigh of relief escaped her lips - the icy blanket of snow that had draped the outdoors had retreated, leaving the ground safe for Dash's morning excursion.

With a cheerful click, she released the door latch, and Dash exploded into the fresh morning air, a bundle of uncontrolled energy. Jane began brewing her morning coffee, the enchanting aroma of hazelnut and Irish cream filling the home with a comforting embrace.

Cradling a steaming mug, Jane was wrapped in the previous night's dream, a chilling narrative that stirred anxiety. A wave of nausea swept her, and she understood the need to regain control over her spiraling emotions.

She retreated to the sanctuary of her bathroom. Seated on the porcelain throne, fully clothed, she cradled her head. A strange sensation of pinpricks crawled up her fingers as if minute shards of glass were navigating through her veins. Beads of sweat dotted her hairline, and she focused on stabilizing her erratic breathing.

She clenched and unclenched her fists repetitively and wiggled her toes, a seemingly futile attempt at control but a natural response to her escalating stress. Her vision dimmed, the room losing its color and definition until an impenetrable blackness swallowed it.

She swayed, toppling over to strike her head against the cold, unforgiving edge of the bathtub. As she lay unconscious, blood began to pool on the sterile tiles.

An unending stretch of hours faded before Jane clawed back to consciousness, her skull pulsating with a ceaseless, searing pain. The dam of pent-up stress and depression had burst without an explanation, leaving her emotionally exhausted.

Thirst clawed at her throat, propelling her into the kitchen, where she reached for a glass, her fingers quivering like aspen leaves in the wind.

As she filled the glass, her gaze wandered to the window above her sink, where a perplexing reflection snagged her attention. Jane leaned in for a closer inspection, and a sudden bark abruptly pierced the silence. The unexpected sound jolted her, causing her grasp to weaken.

The glass hurtled towards the floor, shattering into a constellation of shards amidst an ever-widening pool of water. "Damn it!" she yelled, the simmering frustration finally boiling. "Another mess for me to clean up."

Muttering an inventory of exasperation under her breath, she armed herself with the broom, dutifully swept up the glittering fragments, then mopped up the spill with a hastily grabbed towel. The conflicting symphony of shattered glass had sent Dash, her usually brave companion, fleeing from the room.

Jane peered around the corner, searching for her terrified pup. Her attention was involuntarily drawn toward her husband's workroom. The door, usually a firm barrier, was slightly ajar, revealing a glimpse of the room's concealed interior.

Venturing into the workspace, she was welcomed by the sight of Dash, his tail wagging like a metronome beneath the safety of the desk. As she knelt to extend a comforting hand toward him, her fingers brushed against a stray piece of wood. Absent-mindedly, she tugged at it, only to be taken aback when a manila folder, previously hidden, tumbled out of its covert spot and landed at her feet.

As Dash scampered out of the room, Jane's curiosity piqued. She picked up the folder and flicked on the nearby desk lamp, casting a soft glow over its contents.

The folder appeared to have been recently rifled through, with the November deadline smudging the inside of the cover. But the faded lettering, almost like a company symbol, caught her eye. She strained to make out the letters, her mind racing through possibilities.

Jane felt an overwhelming sense of unease as she pondered at the documents. It had been months since her husband, John, had disappeared, and the room held too many memories of him. She carefully replaced the folder on the desk and retreated from the room, her head swimming with questions and doubts.

Jane went to the kitchen tremblingly and splashed her face with icy water. As she gazed into the mirror, she couldn't shake the feeling that she was descending a dangerous path, one that would lead her to uncover the truth about John's disappearance, no matter the cost.

The urgent, frenzied scrape of Dash's claws against the door sliced into the steady drone of the sink's rushing water. The rancid stench of decaying waste drifting from the disposal assaulted Jane's senses, causing her face to scrunch in distaste as she fought to suppress the rising urge to vomit. Whirling around, streams of water streaking from her chin, she barely registered Dash's blur of movement as he streaked past her, disappearing into the infringing darkness.

Jane's confusion was etched on her face. Why was Dash so desperate to go outside when he usually avoided it? Ignoring the chill of the frost on her bare feet, she shuffled around the corner and found Dash using all his might to dig into the side of the house. She attempted to stop him, but his size overpowered her, and she felt the sheer strength of his resistance.

The potential harm to the house's foundation began to chew at Jane's peace of mind. "Do you want a treat?" she called out in a falsely cheerful tone, rattling the treat bag to lure Dash from his relentless excavation.

However, Dash remained undiscouraged, his eyes ablaze with uncharacteristic enthusiasm. Plagued by frustration and the biting cold, Jane hurried inside to retrieve a flashlight and shoes before venturing into the unforgiving chill.

An unsettling silence, as reflective as the dark, blanketed the surroundings, disrupted only by the crisp crunch of frost beneath her shoes. The flashlight's beam scoured the area, yet it failed to locate Dash.

As the seconds ticked by, Jane's confusion mounted, her heart pounding a heavy rhythm of uncertainty. "Dash?" she ventured, her voice echoing in the black void. Yet, her call was met with an eerie silence. Where could he have disappeared to?

As Jane stepped into the yawning chasm that had opened up against the very foundation of her home, her heart hammered against her ribcage in a frantic rhythm. The rich scent of freshly turned earth flooded her senses, making her head reel in a disorienting dance.

She paused, steadying herself against the swelling wave of vertigo, attempting to process the surreal scene that confronted her. No prior experience or expectation could have braced her for the monumental challenge ahead; the depths to which Dash had managed to dig in such a brief span were nothing short of astonishing.

Bowing her head to fit under the house's low clearance, Jane extended her arm, the flashlight clutched in her hand, her surrogate eyes piercing the consuming darkness ahead. Her foot squished into the spongy, moisture-infused soil, chilling wetness seeping into her footwear.

Claustrophobia, like a ravenous beast, began to bite at the corners of her psyche. Still, she steeled herself, refusing to succumb to its paralyzing grip.

"There's no turning back now, Jane," she murmured, her voice shaky in the oppressive void. The underpass, as narrow as a constricting windpipe, barely accommodated her frame, forcing her into a hunched posture like an ape.

As she pressed forward, the mud seemed to rise in a silent rebellion, creeping higher until it reached her chest. "Keep going, Jane. You've got this," she muttered, her words serving as a self-spoken mantra against the mounting dread. "You've faced worse and survived. You can do this too."

In a frenzy of fear and desperation, Jane flung her arms about, her hands clawing through the darkness in a frantic search for a lifeline. The struggle to keep her head above the rising tide of mud was becoming increasingly daunting, the viscous sludge infiltrating her nostrils and threatening to choke her.

The soil now lapped at her neck, and a morbid acceptance began to seep into her consciousness - she might perish in the very home she'd built. "At least they won't have far to go for my burial," she thought, a morbid sense of humor surfacing among her desperation.

Yet, a bolt of hope electrified her spirit when her fingers grazed against something firm amid the mud. "Hang in there, Dash," she gasped aloud, the thought of her missing companion fueling her determination. The soil seemed to loosen its grip as she painstakingly hauled herself toward the object.

Still, paradoxically, she felt herself pulled deeper into the mud. Breathless, short gasps tore from her throat as she battled to keep her head above the ground.

Finally, her fingers clamped onto the object with a triumphant yank, pulling herself up. She emerged from the mud-caked darkness, hacking and spitting, her relief as deep as the mud clung to her.

The viscous mud inched relentlessly up to her chin, sealing her in its cold, clammy grasp. Jane found herself yearning for a reunion with John. As she readied herself for the impending suffocation, an unexpected chill breezed over her toes, sparking a glimmer of hope within her. She puzzled over the source of this chilling caress and hoped it might signify a pocket of air large enough to sustain her.

As the mud continued its advancement, she glided through it with almost effortless ease, like the smooth passage of someone benefiting from a high-fiber diet. Taking a deep breath, she was swallowed whole by the unforgiving ground.

Her conscious mind dissolved into a tapestry of bizarre hallucinations. At the same time, her spirit seemed to drift toward a holy realm. A tranquil serenity washed over her, like standing on the threshold of an incredible journey.

Was this the prelude to her transcendence into the afterlife? Jane found herself resigned to the belief that she had met her end and had long since surrendered to her fate.

What felt like an eternity stretched before her, yet her eyes opened in a sudden spark of awareness. A wave of recognition washed over her, a powerful realization that she was, against all odds, still among the living! She was a husk of her former self, drained and feeble after the physical and emotional ordeal of her near-death experience.

Recognizing the urgent need to replenish her depleted energy reserves, she decided to pause, rest, and recharge her internal battery before daring to venture further on this seemingly impossible journey.

Stirring from her temporary slumber, Jane was adrift in a sea of disorientation, her body battered and bruised from the ordeal. Her skin was cloaked in mud from head to toe, stemming a less-than-pleasant odor that curled her nose in distaste.

It took her a few moments to register that she was no longer trapped in the mud but had been deposited onto a surface that was both cold and unyieldingly firm, now bearing the imprint of her mud-clad form.

Above her, droplets of water were trickling down, their cold touch splattering against her skin in a rhythm as steady as a metronome. The blackness was so dense that it was impossible to discern the height of the ceiling, which heightened her bewilderment regarding the depth of her fall.

Recalling the purpose of her subterranean venture, she called out for Dash. Her voice barely penetrated the enclosing silence, and her call for her beloved pet was met with extreme quiet. It was so silent that she could hear her heartbeat pounding in her ears.

Paralyzed by the enormity of her predicament, Jane found her flashlight absent, a crucial tool lost to the depths.

Yet, the sensation of a breeze ghosting across her skin offered a glimmer of hope. The tunnel must have an entrance and an exit. But which way should she go? Lost in contemplation, she weighed her options, understanding that her decision could drastically influence her chances of survival.

Jane's mind stumbled upon a memory of John, engrossed in a video game on his PlayStation 3 several years prior. The narrative revolves around a serial killer, a series of trials, and a relentless downpour of rain. John's affection for the game had bordered on an obsession.

Jane recalled a scene with remarkable clarity: a middle-aged protagonist navigating a tortuous tunnel strewn with shards of glass, the flickering flame of a match serving as his only guide.

The scientific rationale behind the scenes eluded her. Still, she felt an odd sense of gratitude that her current predicament did not involve a gantlet of sharp glass.

While she could not light a match or spontaneously combust, she did have one essential guide: the wind. With the subtle nudge of the cool breeze at her back, she was compelled to follow its direction, a silent whisper in the darkness guiding her through her subterranean landscape.

Jane could hear the beating echo of her blood coursing through her veins. Her heart pounded a disconnected rhythm, the tempo accelerating alarmingly. She resented how her anxiety heightened her bodily awareness, forcing her to keep a mental tally of her heartbeats, reaching an unsettling 140 BPM even as she moved at a measured pace.

"Easy, Jane, easy," she murmured, her voice shaky in the enveloping darkness. She attempted to distract her mind from the invading claustrophobia, focusing on trivial mental gymnastics, an attempt to untangle her thoughts from the panic clawing at her sanity.

Her instincts, honed by years of survival, pricked at her consciousness, urging her to tread cautiously. The risk of colliding with a hidden wall or stumbling into an unseen abyss or chasm could render her stranded and helpless in this underground maze. "One step at a time, Jane," she coached herself, "You've got this. Just breathe and keep moving."

Lost within a void of endless obscurity, each passing moment a haunting echo of her solitude. Her stomach growled with the intensity of a caged beast, a harsh reminder of her mortal bounds, its instinctual protest against the deprivation of sustenance.

The air around her stirred, a subtle breeze gradually gaining strength as she delved into the unknown, seemingly the only friend in her solitary journey. The pitch-black darkness presented no variations of light, no comforting silhouettes, nor shimmering glimmers of hope, just an infinite expanse of consuming blackness.

Amid her grim contemplation, her foot squelched against something soft and warmer than the cold, hard ground. An overpowering, foul odor immediately invaded her senses, a nauseating stench of decay and filth.

"This is dog crap!" Jane blurted out, a mixture of disgust and relief washing over her. She scraped her shoe against the rugged surface, attempting to rid herself of the unpleasant substance. Despite the gross encounter, this was a sign that she was not wholly lost. She was moving forward, albeit mindlessly, in some direction.

"Dash!" She yelled into the void, her voice echoing back to her, a haunting reminder of her solitude. The only response was her voice bouncing back at her. But she held on to the hope that her journey was not in vain, that she was making progress, however small, within this seemingly endless darkness.

Jane continued to move forward, wondering how long it would take her to be completely blinded by the pure darkness. The breeze came from her right, so she adjusted her course counterclockwise to follow it.

As the current grew weaker, figuring out which way to go became harder. Her hands eventually became her guide, and three steps later, she found herself at a dead end. She explored the wall blocking her escape with her hands, seeing it made of smooth plywood, reeking of either oak or maple.

There were no splinters to be found, and the wall was so soft she could even rub it. With no more breeze to guide her, she used her instincts and turned right, moving in a circular direction.

She was instantly struck by the realization that something she had previously deemed impossible had occurred - her hands were now entirely visible to her. *Where was this light coming from?* She wondered.

As Jane adjusted to the overwhelming darkness, she found her eyes drawn to a pinprick of warm, orange light from a small window to her right. It was a light beacon that fluttered like a lone firefly in the surrounding blackness, its subtle glow seemingly higher than her current ground level, a hint that she was indeed descending.

Intrigued, she murmured to herself, "What could that be?" A sense of curiosity began to replace her initial fear. The light was minuscule, but it felt like a lighthouse guiding lost ships through a stormy night in this darkness. With newfound determination, she took a step toward the light.

However, her sudden movement was abruptly halted as a sharp pain shot through her foot. "Ouch!" she yelped, hopping on one foot. Her toes had collided with an unexpected, solid metal object lurking invisibly in her path. She crouched down, her fingers delicately exploring the thing that had been the source of her sudden agony.

"Interesting," she mused. The pain was momentarily forgotten as her fingertips traced the cold, rugged outline of the object. A strange encounter in the dimness piqued her curiosity even more. Despite her current predicament, Jane was drawn to the mystery, each discovery a spark of intrigue in an otherwise daunting journey.

At long last, Jane stood before the source of the tiny, shimmering light, the mysterious object just within reach of her outstretched fingers. She touched what felt like a Plexiglas window, a cold, smooth surface familiar to her touch. Her hand moved in recurring circles, wiping away the thick dust and grime that had settled over time.

The texture beneath her fingers became warm and moist as she rubbed, her effort rewarded as the light gradually grew brighter, casting a weak glow that stretched a few feet into the surrounding darkness.

The dim light revealed her clothing, tattered and torn, a tribute to her harrowing journey. Despite her scruffy appearance, Jane remained undiscouraged. Her attention was riveted solely on the bright light and its compelling mystery. Her gaze returned to the window, the orange hue diffusing through the Plexiglas, bathing her immediate surroundings in a warm, soothing glow.

As her eyes adjusted to the new light, she noticed more details. A circular steel hatch was attached to the glass window, bejeweled with several mechanical rotary wheels. The soft orange light reflected off the metallic surface, casting a hunter-green hue.

However, it could have been standard gray or army brown under average daylight. An intriguing thought crossed her mind,

"Could this be an old army bunker from one of the wars?" she wondered aloud. "But what the heck is it doing under my house?"

Despite the question, nothing about the hatch suggested it was a relic of a departed era; it didn't bear the coat of age or the weathered look of neglect. It could have been freshly painted, and its surface smooth and well-maintained.

Now a burning flame, Jane's curiosity overpowered all her other senses. The mystery of what lay beyond the hatch consumed her thoughts, overshadowing her physical discomfort and the fear of the unknown.

Now, nothing else mattered more than uncovering the secrets inside the bunker. The world outside ceased to exist for her, and the hatch became her sole focus, a cryptic puzzle demanding her undivided attention.

Jane extended her hand, her fingers closing around one of the wheels, the gateway to an unfamiliar world. However, she felt something unusual as her fingers traced the metallic surface. The latch bore tiny indentations and scratches, patterns that were strangely reminiscent of teeth marks.

"Could this be Dash's work?" Jane wondered aloud, her voice a mere whisper in the stillness. It didn't seem like a hasty, one-time job; instead, the latch was gnawed on repeatedly, the metal surface dented and scratched in several places as if subjected to a persistent onslaught.

Her mind raced with the implications. Dash had been here before, not just passing through but actively trying to pry open this metallic barrier. The idea made her chuckle as she visualized Dash, her loyal companion, struggling with his lack of opposable thumbs, attempting desperately to unlock this hatch.

"Would you have offered me as a sacrifice to the pig gods for thumbs, Dash?" She mused aloud, a whimsical smile tugging at her lips. The situation's absurdity was not lost, and she questioned her sanity. The thought of her dog attempting to open a bunker was ludicrous. Yet, the evidence lay before her, a witness to a reality stranger than fiction.

Despite the gravity of her situation, Jane couldn't help but let out a low, hearty chuckle. A smirk played on her face, her eyes sparkling with amusement as she imagined Dash, the canine locksmith. This spark of humor kept her grounded and her spirit unbroken in a world of uncertainty.

Jane's hands, smeared with dirt and grime, cradled her face as she curled into a protective ball, her body echoing the vulnerability she felt within. Tears welled in her eyes, their path blocked by the mud streaked across her cheeks, a physical barrier to her emotional release.

The quiet was shattered by rapid, shallow breaths, causing Jane to snap out of her trance. Whirling around, she noticed a peculiar, ominous shadow. It was elusive and undefined, a spectral presence that stirred her curiosity again.

As she moved closer, her hand tentatively stretched out to touch the shadowy figure. Still, it dissolved into the darkness, retreating into a small, hidden crawlspace just as she was about to connect.

A sense of reluctance washed over her as she stared into the mysterious hole's mouth. She sank to her hands and knees, her heart pounding as she peered into the intriguing void. Her mind raced with thoughts of the elusive entity she had almost touched. What was it? Why did it retreat?

However, her contemplation was abruptly interrupted by a familiar sound, a sharp "Woof!" that echoed through the silence. The pleasant and comforting sound momentarily pushed away her fears and uncertainties, replacing them with a surge of hope and intrigue. Yet again, Jane was left wondering about the mysteries of the darkness.

A surge of adrenaline coursed through Jane's veins, making her heart flutter like it was about to burst out of her chest. The color drained from her face, leaving her skin a pale shade barely discernible in the dim light. However, as the initial shock subsided, she regained her composure, her frantic heartbeat gradually slowing down.

The sight before her eyes brought a rush of relief – it was only Dash, standing there with his usual canine innocence. "For Christ's sake, Dash!" She exclaimed, her voice a mix of relief, frustration, and exasperation. Her eyes softened as she looked at her companion, but her voice still trembled with the residual fear.

"I almost died trying to find you!" she continued, letting out a shaky breath. Her words echoed in the silence of the bunker, a testament to the ordeal she had just gone through. Despite her relief at finding Dash, she couldn't hide her frustration – the fear she had experienced was real, and the scars would likely last a while.

Yet, in the face of Dash's innocent gaze, her anger quickly faded, replaced by a sense of gratitude. They were together again, and that was all that mattered for now. But she couldn't help but add, "You owe me big time, buddy," a hint of a smile playing on her lips as she reached out to pat Dash's head.

Dash stood before her, his coat matted with grime, his eyes unflinchingly meeting hers. His gaze had a familiarity, a shared understanding that only comes from shared experiences. Then, without warning, he broke the intense eye contact and darted towards the engulfing darkness, his figure disappearing within seconds before Jane could muster a call to halt him.

With a sense of urgency, Jane followed in the direction Dash had vanished into, finding herself before the small, ominous hole she had spotted earlier. Could this be their only escape route? With the hatch stubbornly refusing to budge, this hidden passage was her last resort.

"Wh-Where are you going? Do you know the way out? Dash!" She questioned the space she was in - her supply of air, the potential for entrapment. With no access to food, water, or shelter, survival seemed a far-fetched dream.

Her mind was a battlefield - would she risk starvation and dehydration to confront her deepest fears, or would she succumb to the impending doom? Darwin's survival of the fittest theory resonated with her now more than ever. The choice was hers to yield to her fears and accept her fate or fight back for a glimmer of hope.

Before committing to her decision, she cast one last glance at the cryptic hatch. "I can't leave without knowing what this thing is." Striding over, she positioned herself before the rusted wheel. Her teeth gnashed together, and she summoned every bit of her strength, attempting to force the hatch open.

The first attempt was unsuccessful, her palms raw with fresh blisters. Undeterred, she gave it another try, but the hatch remained unyielding, seemingly mocking her desperate efforts. She felt around the surface area of the hatch and felt intricate markings that may require a key or sequence of levers.

She vowed to return better prepared and keep a closer watch on Dash, her seemingly adventurous guard dog. Despite the adversity, Jane's spirit remained unbroken - her will to survive ignited a fire of determination.

Jane's body trembled with fear as she crept toward the crawl space. The darkness seemed to swallow her whole as she positioned herself to fit through the narrow opening. With each inch she crawled, the walls closed around her, squeezing the air from her lungs.

Her head plunged into the hole, and the light vanished as she wriggled deeper. The mud was slick and slimy, making traction difficult. Her muscles burned with exertion as she contorted to the tight space. Panic threatened to overwhelm her as she realized she was running out of air.

A shroud of impenetrable darkness swallowed her whole, stealing away her vision and leaving her in a world devoid of light. The mud clinging to her arms and legs was heavy, like shackles binding her, making each attempt at movement a superhuman task. She felt an unnerving pressure surrounding her wrists, tightening its grip with every passing moment.

She could feel her arm being jerked forward with each brutal tug, each one more forceful than the last, the violent pulls threatening to tear her limb from its socket.

Jane wobbled on the cliff of unconsciousness, her body succumbing to the suffocating lack of oxygen. The sensation of her arm wrenched away was excruciating, a searing pain that seemed to rip through her—one violent jerk, two, three, then a momentary pause in the onslaught.

Suddenly, with a final, monstrous tug, she was expelled from the suffocating darkness into the open air. The abrupt transition was jarring, a violent catapult from the clutches of despair into the arms of freedom, a journey marked by relentless struggle and unbearable pain.

A rush of cool air filled her lungs as Jane gasped desperately, each breath a lifeline as she clung to consciousness. Her body quivered, shaking from the shock of her ordeal, her every nerve screaming in protest. She lay there for a few agonizing minutes, her mind a whirlwind of confusion and disorientation as she attempted to comprehend her situation.

With a monumental effort, she attempted to move, only to be met with a chilling realization. Her right side was numb, unresponsive to her attempts to stir it into action. Her arm felt alien, detached, and her fingers barely twitched in response to her commands.

"No, no, no!" Jane's voice echoed in the desolate expanse, her words a harsh, terrified whisper in the quiet. Terror washed over her as she realized the horrific truth - her arm had been pulled from its socket.

"I can't... I can't believe this...Oh boy, this is bad," she murmured, her voice a feeble whisper among the pain. The gravity of her situation dawned on her, a grim reality that threatened to engulf her in a wave of despair. She was in dire straits, her body mutilated, her chances of survival dwindling with each passing moment.

Jane opened her eyes to the sight of an amber-glowing lantern, her face flat against the soil. She struggled to comprehend what had happened, and her vision was still blurry from the shock. It was like the effects of downing a fifth of Jack after a night of poor decisions - only without the comforting thought of sleep to buffer the hangover.

Jane forced herself onto her knees, her kneecaps sinking into the damp mud, and felt an alarming lack of movement in her arm. She was no doctor and had not experienced a dislocation before, but a memory from her childhood came to mind.

Jane's dad had always been a source of warmth and love, his soft nature comforting in their household. But when Jane's mom passed away, it hit him hard. The loss threw him into a bottomless pit of sadness that he couldn't escape. To cope with his grief, he turned to drugs and alcohol, hoping they'd help him escape the constant, gut-wrenching pain he felt.

However, this misguided diversion only served to amplify his anguish, mutating it into a destructive force that wreaked havoc on his life. His previously calm demeanor was replaced by an unpredictable temper, a volatile storm that raged without warning.

Jane tolerated the force of his emotional turmoil, finding herself at the receiving end of his unpredictable outbursts. The transformation was heartrending, a grim testament to the devastating power of loss.

Among this rowdy period, a new figure emerged in Jane's life - her stepmother. She was a beacon of strength and independence, a woman with an unyielding spirit and a heart brimming with compassion. Recognizing the deep-seated pain that Jane and her father were grappling with, she stepped into their lives, determined to change.

The initial phase was a welcome respite. Jane's stepmother introduced a sense of stability that their lives had been sorely missing, a comforting routine among the chaos. Jane found solace in her presence, a maternal figure that filled the void left by her mother's departure.

However, time unveiled an unsettling transformation. The once strong, compassionate woman started showing signs of instability, her demeanor marred by sudden fits of anger and violent outbursts. She would explode at Jane's father without warning, her words cutting through the tense silence like a knife. The bruises on his arms stood testimony to her violent inclinations, and the fear that flickered in his eyes was a heartbreaking sight for Jane.

Her father attempted to sever the ties bound him to this volatile relationship, but his efforts proved ineffective. Her stepmother had a manipulative grip on him, pulling him back each time he tried to break away.

One fateful day, their turmoil-ridden domestic scene climaxed. A heated argument escalated rapidly, with Jane's stepmother lunging at her father in a blind rage. But instead of connecting with its intended target, her fist met the delicate glass figure of a duck. This object has captivated Jane's imagination since she was a child.

The force of the blow dislocated her stepmother's arm, prompting a scream so piercing it seemed to shatter the remaining silence in their home.

A wave of anger washed over Jane, a fierce protective instinct rising within her towards her struggling father. "I'll call the police!" she had cried, her voice shaking with fear and determination. She was ready to reach out for help, to end this cycle of violence that had consumed their lives.

Yet, her father had stopped her, his voice low and strained. "No, Jane," his eyes reflected fear and concern. "I can't risk it... I can't leave you alone." His past encounters with the law cast a long, intimidating shadow, threatening to tear him away from his daughter. Even amidst the chaos, his foremost concern was Jane's well-being, proof of the depth of his love for her.

So, they sat there silently as her stepmother cried out in pain. The shattered glass duck symbolized everything that had gone wrong in their lives, and Jane knew that things would never be the same again.

The memory of that day, burdened with emotion and conflict, was etched deeply into Jane's heart.

Jane watched as her father worked quickly and efficiently to care for her stepmother's injury. She was amazed at his resourcefulness and skill, making her wonder if there was more to him than his struggles with addiction and anger.

Over the next few weeks, Jane's father became her stepmother's primary caregiver, tending to her every need and ensuring she was comfortable. He cooked her meals, helped her bathe, and even drove her to her physical therapy appointments. It was a side of him that Jane hadn't seen in years, giving her hope that he could change.

As her stepmother's arm gradually mended in the quiet aftermath of the storm, a new chapter unfolded in Jane's life. Her father, who had often concealed his emotions behind a hardened facade, began to unravel his vulnerabilities before her. His voice, once a mere whisper amidst the chaos, now echoed with the haunting tales of his struggles.

"I've battled with addiction, Jane," he confessed, each word heavy with regret and raw honesty that Jane had never witnessed before. His eyes filled with a potent mix of pain and remorse. "After your mother... I hit rock bottom."

His admissions were not just confessions but also acknowledgments of his mistakes. He expressed his regret for the anguish he had inadvertently inflicted upon their family, his words an emotional testament to his inner torment.

This heart-to-heart conversation marked a pivotal point in their relationship. Jane began to see her father beyond the veil of his mistakes. He was not just a man battling his demons but also a father capable of unconditional love and compassion.

As the weeks metamorphosed into months, a subtle transformation occurred in their fractured family. Jane's father continued to tend to her stepmother's needs, and, in doing so, their bond began to strengthen.

It was a challenging journey, riddled with anger and frustration, yet they persevered. They were two broken souls mending their lives, healing their wounds together, their shared struggles forging an unanticipated bond amidst the challenges.

Reflecting upon that day, Jane recognized it as a defining moment in their lives. The shattered glass duck, an emblem of her childhood fascination, had ironically transformed into a touching symbol of their collective pain and struggle. It silently witnessed their journey, its fragmented pieces mirroring their shattered lives.

Yet, the shattered duck had served as an unexpected catalyst for the confusion and despair. It had shattered the barriers of silence and denial that had enveloped them, forcing them to confront the reality of their circumstance. The incident, painful as it was, had sparked a wave of change, pushing them towards a path of healing and reconciliation.

Over time, they had emerged from the wreckage, scarred but resilient. The adversity had not torn them apart but brought them closer, forging bonds tested in the crucible of their shared struggles.

As Jane navigated her current predicament, she drew strength from these memories. Her past trials served as a potent reminder of her innate resilience. She was a survivor, shaped by her experiences, and each challenge was a stepping stone propelling her toward a future filled with hope and resolve.

Jane was trapped in an all-too-familiar dilemma, her survival hinging on her resourcefulness. She drew in a deep, shuddering breath, each molecule of oxygen becoming a silent prayer for courage and strength. With her heart pounding a persistent tempo against her ribcage, she attempted to mimic her father's actions.

Darkness seized her again, a sinister curtain falling over her consciousness. Her world spiraled into a void, where reality morphed into a sinister dreamscape. Jane was plunged into a nightmare of a nightmare, her body a wooden statue, a prisoner chained by invisible shackles, unable to escape the horrors of her mind.

# 8

Out of the womb, he was born in a sinister light. Feet first and skin as soft as the steel of a scythe. He screamed and cried out, met by the slap of a latex hand. Marked by the dangling of a limp skin particle, he was beautiful.

The man in the white coat summoned the nurse to take him away to be incubated. This 3-month premature baby had slim odds of survival, with time running out. On the scale, he only weighed 3 lbs. and 3oz.; he needed intensive care from someone other than his mother. She was a slender, tall woman with golden blonde hair and a crooked smile. The father, as always, was late to the delivery of his fourth child, only managing to be present for one of his children at the time of labor. He may have been a good dad, but he was undeniably selfish.

When he received the call from work, he arrived with his three other boys, unable to wrap his head around his wife's early departure. But when he entered the room, she was nowhere to be found. The doctor then explained that his wife had experienced complications and underwent cardiac arrest during the delivery, resulting in internal bleeding and subsequent loss of consciousness.

It was too late after a half hour of trying to revive her. Dad's single tear spoke volumes as he was informed of the devastating news. His two younger sons were still too young to comprehend the gravity of the situation. He walked over to the incubation table and gazed down upon his newborn son. He couldn't help but sense a mixture of sorrow and love for this little life, which he could only view as the source of such tragedy.

The autopsy was performed in a cold and blinding room at the bottom of the hospital. When the whirring blade touched the sternum, Jacen's mother's warmth infiltrated the room as if her soul were being liberated from her lifeless body.

The autopsy results were in, and her cause of death had been determined to be a brain aneurism. As the father read the report, he knew that congenital disabilities and aneurysms should not be correlated. Something was amiss, and he had no clue what it could be.

Grief-stricken, the father had been at the hospital for days, vigilantly monitoring his newborn son's tenuous chances of survival after his wife's sudden passing. Standing by the infant's bedside, he came across a paper with a name scrawled on it - Jacen. Baffled, he wondered if his wife had mentioned it before her body was laid to rest.

Three weeks passed, and baby Jacen was still in the hospital. The doctor told his dad he could be taken home in the coming days. It was also assumed that considering his size and how premature he was, Jacen was fortunate to be alive and had shown remarkable resilience against illnesses. Jacen had had pneumonia earlier in the week and strep throat, yet he was still going strong.

The father was overjoyed to take his son home and reunite him with the rest of the family, vigilant that he would remain safe and sound. Upon weighing Jacen, the doctor beamed with pride at the impressive 6 lbs. and 2oz. he had gained since birth. With a satisfied nod, the doctor remarked on the healthy weight gain and reassured the father that Jacen was doing wonderfully.

Jacen grew into a toddler in three years, walking and speaking a few words. The dad was still mourning his wife but had re-married a much younger woman, half his age. The other boys were still adjusting to a new woman in the house, and her presence always seemed a source of tension. She would stay home with the boys while their dad worked, and with the summer holidays in full swing, there appeared to be endless time and possibilities. Caring for four boys alone was daunting enough to drive anyone insane!

Jacen was coloring the table with his crayons, scribbling away like any other child. Yet he only seemed to use black. One could almost see the potential of the soft white paper and all the different colors that could have been expressed with a bit of imagination.

Unfortunately, his artwork ended up on the lovely magnolia table, and his new stepmother noticed. She grabbed him by the arm and spoke in a voice filled with anger and frustration, though he showed no emotion and seemed unafraid. When she realized she wasn't getting her point across, she shouted a demand to send him to his room. She then grabbed him by his blonde, curly hair, shoving him into his room and slamming the door shut.

Jacen crawled into bed and closed his eyes, not knowing what was happening. He recalled the situation and felt her saliva and coffee breath on his tiny face. A wave of anger grew inside him, a feeling he hadn't experienced before. He eventually drifted off, and darkness enveloped the room.

Whispers and shadows filled the air, and a red, translucent fabric descended from the sky, trapping him. Two white legs appeared from the material, along with a torso, arms, and a head. It was his stepmother, her eyes burning with rage, and her mouth opened wide in a shout. She grabbed him by the hair, causing him pain. He desperately attempted to stop her, grabbed her mouth, and clamped his fingers on two of her teeth. He felt his fingers close together and the taste of thick, dark red blood trickling down his arm.

Jacen awoke an hour later, his fist clenched and his baby teeth grinding together. His fear ran through him like a cold shock, and he curiously approached the door. It had been opened, and he stepped into the living room. His stepmom lay on the couch, still and unmoving. He walked over and tapped her head, but there was no response. He grabbed her by the hair and pulled it towards him.

Suddenly, warm thick blood scattered across his face, and Jacen noticed her eyelids had been severed off. Two teeth were missing and replaced by two long rusted nails entering her brain from the left and right side. Jacen was the last thing she saw before she passed away in a brain-dead state.

Jacen stumbled out to the park, his clothes stained with blood. His brothers, playing in the small open space, stopped when they saw him, and the oldest ran up to him, horrified. He quickly called for an ambulance, and when it arrived, the paramedic noticed a young woman's corpse. It was clear from the nature of her death that it was a murder.

The dad arrived home and was bombarded with questions before he could comprehend what was happening. His heart sank when he saw his new wife sprawled out on the couch, her eyes bulging.

He collapsed in shock and disbelief at what he had seen. His alibi of being at work had been disproved, and the only proof the police had was of a toddler covered in the victim's blood. There was no sign of forced entry or any other indication that someone else had been in the house.

The dad glared at Jacen and grabbed him by the shoulders, shaking him violently and yelling, "What did you do? You murdered your mother and your stepmother, you little monster!"

He thought, my son is a serial killer and hasn't even turned five yet.

Jacen looked at his father and said wryly, "She's not my mother; she was the lady in red. I don't have a mother; I killed her by invading her body and clotting her blood, causing the inside of her brain to explode. Is that what you told me, Dad? I can hear you say it in your nightmares."

When Jacen sleeps, his mother rises in her devilish apparel to take what was rightfully hers. He knows her better than anyone else, so Jacen was brought to a psychiatric hospital named Slit Haven to determine if a toddler could commit such a gruesome act. On his first night there, he dreamt of himself and his mother alone in the backyard of their house.

He looked over and saw his father trying to bludgeon his mother with a lampshade, and she scrambled to the kitchen to arm herself. Her other sons were there too, wearing grotesque masks resembling a bloody caricature of Bill Murray.

She let out a loud yet soft wail, trapped with nowhere to turn. Suddenly, the father and boys collapsed as wild boars devoured their bodies.

She took no effort to save them, walking back outside covered in their blood and hugging Jacen. "It's just you and me now, baby like it should have been long ago. Nobody can hurt you anymore; I love you, Jacen."

"I love you too, Mommy," he whispered as she disappeared. His shirt had two bloody handprints on the back, and without thinking, he grabbed a fork from his last meal and jammed it into his temple. His soul lifted into the air, and halfway up in the sky, he held his mom's hand and smiled.

"We're home."

# 9

With a sudden, violent start, Jane was thrust back awake. It was as if her soul, having wandered in the wilderness of her nightmares, was yanked abruptly back into the confines of her physical form. A gasp tore from her lips, the first breath of her new reality tasting sharp and sterile.

She found herself in a room crammed with intense brightness that seemed to pierce her soul, making her squint. The room was a direct contrast to the dark hole of her dreams, as blinding as the sun after a long, moonless night.

The air was thick with a unique scent that was comforting and disturbing. It smelled of a nursing home, a mingling of antiseptic cleanliness, faded flowers, and the underlying, inescapable note of age and frailty.

Intertwined with this was the abundant odor of hand sanitizer, its robust and alcohol-based aroma a grim reminder of her current predicament.

As Jane attempted to lift her head, a dull throb echoed through her skull, each pulse a painful reminder of her recent ordeal. Her muscles protested, heavy and sluggish as if bound by unseen weights. The soft rustle of movement reached her ears, followed by a voice, gentle yet firm.

"Ma'am, I need you to stay down," the voice implored, a soothing balm on her frayed nerves. The woman's tone was professional yet laced with an underlying concern. "Please, tell me your name," she added.

Jane's mind swam with confusion, the woman's words swirling in the fog of her consciousness. Yet within the disarray, one thing was clear. She was no longer alone, lost in the sea of her nightmares. She was back in the waking world, a reality that was just as daunting yet held the promise of help, of healing.

"Where am I?" Jane's voice was barely a whisper, the words slipping past her lips as her eyes fluttered open.

The figure before her, a police officer named Yolanda, observed her curiously. Her dark eyebrow cocked upward, a silent question mark punctuating the air between them. As she replied, a smirk played on her lips, her voice laced with a hint of dry humor.

"Well, sweetheart, I was hoping you could shed some light on that mystery. You're the one who decided to take an unprepared nap in this hospital bed." Yolanda's badge glistened under the harsh hospital lights as she introduced herself. "I'm Officer Yolanda, your guardian angel for this little adventure of yours."

A groan slipped from Jane's lips as she attempted to sit up, her body protesting the movement. Yolanda's hand was gentle but firm on her shoulder, pushing her back onto the crisp hospital sheets. "Hold on there, Jane Doe. You've had quite a ride. Can you remember anything that might help us piece together this puzzle?"

Jane shook her head, a smirk creasing her features as a jolt of pain seared through her shoulder. "No, nothing. I remember going for a run, and then... I woke up here."

Yolanda's nod was thoughtful, her pen dancing across a clipboard as she recorded Jane's words. "Well, we'll need to take your full statement once you're up for it. But just so you know, it's generally not good practice to be discovered on the pavement outside the hospital nursing a dislocated shoulder."

Jane's eyes rolled heavenward in exasperation. "I- wait, what?" Jane sat there in confusion as she was trying to piece together everything that had happened up to this point. "I don't recall lying on any pavement. And believe me, Officer, dislocating my shoulder wasn't high on my bucket list."

Yolanda's smirk was back, her amusement evident. "Well, aren't you a snappy little thing? I like that. But we'll have to dig deeper into this, Jane Doe. So, for now, rest up and let the medical experts do their work."

As Yolanda turned to leave, Jane couldn't suppress the question that bubbled up. "Wait, Yolanda. What's your theory? What do you think happened to me?"

Yolanda's grin was a flash of white in the sterile room. "Oh, sweetheart. I'm a cop, not a psychic. But if you're looking for wild guesses, I'd say it's either extraterrestrial intervention or one hell of a night gone wrong." Her wink was the last thing Jane saw before Yolanda exited the room, leaving behind a wake of unanswered questions and a whirlwind of possibilities to consider.

Jane's gaze fell downward, her eyes widening slightly at the sight of her attire. She was dressed in a plain hospital robe, its material crisp and clean against her skin, and her feet were snuggly encased in freshly laundered socks. A sudden realization washed over her – *someone had changed her clothes. But who?*

Her attention was drawn to an oddity resting on the bedside table, a peculiar remote shaped like a light bulb. Its distinct feature was a glaring red button - a silent call for assistance. Without a second thought, she reached out, her fingers pressing the button with a dedication born of desperation.

Her call was answered almost immediately. The door swung open to reveal a young nurse, his boyish features packed with concern. He juggled a chart and a basket filled with medical supplies in one hand, his efficiency evident in how he moved.

"Is everything okay?" His words were carefully measured, his tone a soothing blend of reassurance and professionalism.

Jane nodded, her voice barely above a whisper as she replied, "Yeah, I think so."

His next question was standard protocol, "What is your pain level?" As he asked, Jane strained to push her body back, seeking a more comfortable position against the stern hospital bed.

Her frustration found a voice as she pleaded, "Can anyone explain what's happening? I have a skull-splitting headache and can hardly feel anything from the neck down."

The nurse's expression softened, his gaze sympathetic as he recounted the strange tale.

"From what we've pieced together, an SUV screeched to a halt in our emergency lane around midnight. A man in a red jumpsuit and a grey hoodie emerged. He claimed to have found a woman – you - lying unconscious and shivering in the cold. He placed you on the pavement and quickly ran back toward his vehicle. Without wasting a moment, a nurse and two doctors rushed out, loaded you onto a stretcher, and whisked you away for immediate care. But before they could interrogate him further, the man disappeared. He drove off into the night, leaving no trace of his identity."

"So, a stranger deemed it appropriate to scoop me up, deposit me here, and then vanish into the night without a second thought for my wellbeing?" Jane's voice wavered between disbelief and anger. "And to add a cherry on top of this surreal sundae, I was greeted by a police officer hinting at potential foul play."

The nurse's eyes sparkled with a hint of shared amusement as she mentioned Officer Yolanda.

"She might come across as somewhat formidable, but beneath that stern exterior is a heart of gold," he explained. "Once you get

159

past her rough-around-the-edges persona, you'll find she's more bark than bite."

He paused momentarily, his gaze distant before continuing, "As for your mysterious Good Samaritan in the jumpsuit, I'd venture to say he was more guardian angel than an ominous figure. But then again, perceptions vary, don't they?"

The nurse's voice lowered, the levity fading as he added, "The doctor's preliminary examination thankfully ruled out any form of sexual assault. But there's an air of unease, a sense that not all pieces of this puzzle fit together.

"Some detectives have been assigned to your case, and they're eager to speak with you once you feel up to it. Better hurry, though, before those painkillers kick in." His words hung in the air, a sobering reminder of the complexity of Jane's situation.

With a wry smile, Jane said, "Oh lovely, I can't wait." Her eyes rolled with a hint of sarcasm, making it impossible for the nurse to miss.

With a cheerful tone, the nurse said, "All right, I'll let them know you're up and about. Let me know if you need anything else; I'm just a button push away!" He smiled, awaiting Jane's response to his attempt at being lighthearted, but she remained silent. With a slight shrug, the nurse gave a friendly nod and left the room.

Jane had a million thoughts running through her mind from her last two encounters. Yet, she was still distracted from having just gone through a Goonies-style underground adventure beneath her house. She thought, "How could I have been so foolish and naive? I bet John knew about the bunker, and how did Dash even get involved? I forgot about Dash. Is he ok?"

Just as Jane was about to voice a growing worry, her train of thought was derailed by a sudden, sharp rap on the emergency room door. Without waiting for a response, the door swung open, admitting two men dressed in dull attire. They held notepads like shields, their eyes brimming with an almost intense eagerness.

"Good morning, Ma'am. Detectives Riverdale and Piccolo, at your service," they announced, their voices harmonizing in an unintentional duet.

"Can you tell us what day it is?" Jane met their question with silence. "We've spoken to your doctor. He mentioned you might have a concussion," they added, their expressions shifting to concern.

"Feeling pretty good, actually. Woah... this room sure is lovely," Jane retorted, a mischievous smile tugging at her lips. "So, your name's Piccolo? Like the green guy from Dragon Ball Z?" Her eyes danced with amusement as she continued, "My husband... or ex-husband... or rather, late husband, was a big fan of that show."

Jane's speech began to waver, her words slurring together as she continued her nostalgic ramble. "He'd always get so irritated when I confused Piccolo with that other guy, Cell," she added, her voice soft with a hint of affection. "Namek, Namek, Namek, no!"

She shouted, her arms flailing about as she mimicked the animated movements of the show's characters.

Suddenly, her playful demeanor shifted, overtaking her with a wave of emotion. Tears welled up in her eyes and spilled down her cheeks. "They destroyed your home planet!" she cried, her voice trembling with vicarious grief. "I can't believe they'd do such a thing. I'm so sorry for your loss," she managed through her sobs, her earlier wit replaced by a heartfelt sorrow.

"Well, ma'am, it seems the painkillers are certainly doing their magic," one of the detectives quipped, a lighthearted note in his voice. The men exchanged glances, their faces etched with amusement. With a nod, they tucked their notepads into their pockets like magicians finishing their act and approached the exit.

Jane's laughter rang out, a touch of joy sparkling in her eyes. "What on earth are you talking about, Mr. Pickle?" she teased, her words slightly slurred but her wit razor-sharp.

"And while you're at it, give 'King Kai' my regards. And if it's not too much trouble, give that pesky monkey a swift kick in the…butt!" Her voice carried a frisky cadence, even as the edges of her consciousness began to blur.

# 10

Jane stirred from her drug-induced slumber when morning's soft light filtered into the room. Her tired eyes opened to see Officer Yolanda standing by her bed. "Good morning, Sunshine," Yolanda greeted, her lips curling into a smile that didn't quite manage to banish the worry from her eyes.

"I understand your memory's playing 'hide and seek,' but I've still got a job to do," she continued, her tone serious. She held up her badge, allowing the morning sunlight to bounce off its polished surface. "See this? This badge is a symbol of my commitment to your safety. It means I'm dedicated to unraveling what happened to you."

Jane nodded, a faint shiver flowing through her as she was caught in the crosshairs of Yolanda's firm gaze. "All right, I'll do my best to cooperate. But I can't recall anything."

Yolanda exhaled a sigh that seemed to carry the world's weight, her arms crossing over her chest in a defensive stance. "Well, that's just peachy," she muttered, her voice thick with frustration. "You were beaten within an inch of your life and discarded like yesterday's trash. And let's not forget that unholy stench you left behind. I must piece together the puzzle of what happened to you, so your cooperation is invaluable."

Jane cringed, a blush creeping up her cheeks at the mention of the smell. "I apologize for that," she murmured, her eyes discouraged. "Wait, where is Dash?"

"Dash?"

"My Great Dane, I remember him being with me before everything went dark."

"There was nothing mentioned about a dog. I can have another officer check to make sure, but it seems you will be released soon. I'd love to hear more about what happened, though."

"I honestly don't know what happened."

Yolanda leaned in her face inches from Jane's—her expression hardened into an unyielding mask of seriousness. "Look, Jane," she began, her voice a low growl. "I don't have the luxury of time to play guessing games. Your life hung in the balance, and I need to find out what led to that. So, no matter how insignificant it may seem, you must tell me if you remember anything."

Jane nodded, the gravity of Yolanda's words sinking in. "Okay, I understand," her voice steady despite the turmoil. "I remember talking to several detectives but can't recall the conversation."

"What detectives?" she echoed, her eyebrows knitting together in a frown. "As far as I know, I'm the sole officer on your case, Jane. You were probably dreaming."

Caught off guard, Jane fell silent, her brow furrowing as she tried to differentiate between reality and medication-induced fantasy.

"Oh, I see," she said, her voice tinged with uncertainty. "That would explain our animated discussion about Dragon Ball Z and something about King Kai giving a monkey a swift kick. I apologize for the confusion."

A hint of a smile tugged at the corners of Yolanda's mouth, softening her stern facade. "It's all right," she reassured Jane, her voice gentler now.

"Just concentrate on your recovery for now. And do me a favor, no more whimsical tales about cartoon characters, okay?" A lighthearted chuckle, a shared moment of humor amid a grim situation, punctuated her words.

Jane gave a light chuckle and agreed to answer questions.

"Tell me about what you remember from last night," Yolanda urged, her voice steady and calm. Jane hesitated, her mind teetering on the height of truth and fabrication. A primal instinct nudged her towards fakes, a protective shield against potential repercussions. She couldn't fathom why it felt so natural to spin a yarn and keep the prying eyes of the law away from her home and life.

It was John. The mere thought of him potentially being involved in criminal activities sent a cold shiver down her spine. John was as familiar and mysterious as a well-read but obscure book. His routine was a mystery, shrouded in a veil of privacy that Jane had never dared to lift. She felt a twinge of discomfort at the thought of prying and crossing a boundary that John had meticulously drawn.

John was an introverted figure, his room his fortress. He would isolate himself for hours, even days, emerging to meet the demands of his job. His outings were as predictable as clockwork, twice a week, no more, no less. In their silent coexistence, Jane had learned to respect his space. This unspoken agreement kept their relationship devoid of conflict.

But with respect came distance, a gaping emptiness reiterated with the unknown. Jane's life was shattered by the hollow rhythm of John's absences, a silence she struggled to fill. She often found herself conjuring images of what he might be doing, but these were mere shadows of her imagination. John never shared his work life, skillfully evading interactions with his colleagues outside the office.

Jane had accepted this harsh reality, a bitter pill swallowed with resignation. She knew she would never be in the know of John's professional life, a world he had carefully kept separate from their shared existence. Yet, despite this glaring flaw, Jane craved to be a part of John's social sphere. She desired inclusion, a potent aspiration to achieve it at any length.

Jane was in a standoff with the closed door of John's office, a room that might as well have been barricaded with a dark "Condemned" sign hammered into the weathered wood.

The chilling memory of his disappearance haunted her, and she was held captive by her promise to him. Her loyalty to her absent husband had become a commandment ingrained in her psyche.

However, Dash seemed immune to this invisible barrier, persistently scratching at the door as if drawn by a forgotten morsel or some other curiosity out of reach.

The idea of breaching that sacred threshold was enough to ignite a storm of anxiety within her, threatening to drain her already fragile mental reserves. She remained determined despite Dash's increasingly adamant attempts to draw her attention.

She found herself entangled in a nerve-wracking confrontation, seated across from the stern and unyielding figure of Officer Yolanda. An icy film of sweat formed on her forehead under the intense scrutiny of Yolanda's penetrating stare.

"I... I tend to have random panic attacks. I was on a run, and sometimes a panic attack is triggered when I noticed my heart racing. My therapist has a name for it. Anyway, I must have fainted and -" Jane managed to hesitate, her voice wavering in the heavy silence. "I really need to get back and check on my dog. He's been by himself, and I am really worried."

"Thanks, Jane. It ain't much, but it's something. I'll check with the doctors to see if they have evidence you had lost consciousness. That would explain the concussion and dislocated shoulder. Must have been one hell of a fall."

Each thump of her racing heart seemed to echo her deception, amplifying under the relentless gaze of the Officer.

The questions continued relentlessly, each a detailed probe into the events of the previous evening. Jane responded with undecided coherence, striving to maintain a consistent narrative. At the same time, the interrogation room walls seemed to close in around her.

Finally, the barrage of questions ceased. Officer Yolanda, seemingly satisfied, thanked Jane for her cooperation and dismissed her. Jane staggered out, a strange cocktail of relief and guilt churning within her. She knew she had been elsewhere the night before, but the fear of revealing her secret was overwhelming.

172

# 11

As the sun gradually descended below the horizon, casting a serene orange hue across the sky, Jane sought refuge in the comfort of her vehicle. The burden of the previous day's events still clung to her like an invisible cloak, enveloping her in a haze of sorrowful contemplation.

The idea of unburdening her dilemma fluttered on the fringes of her consciousness, yet her self-doubt cast a long shadow over the anticipated skepticism she foresaw from others.

As she neared her house, she felt a tight knot in her stomach and dreaded the worst. What if Dash was lost in the unforgiving wilderness or, worse yet, no longer alive? Her heart beat like a war drum, and her anxiety peaked as she opened the door. However, her worries were put to rest as she saw Dash sound asleep on the couch.

Suddenly, Dash's tail thumped to life, beating against the hardwood floor. His ears perked up, swiveling towards her like satellite dishes homing in on a distant signal. The corners of his mouth curled upward into a doggy smile, his tongue lolling out in panting joy.

"Jane," Dash's eyes seemed to say, an ocean of emotion in those gleaming orbs. His excitement was evident; he pranced around her, his claws clicking on the floor in a tap dance of relief.

"I thought you were gone," Jane murmured, her fingers threading through Dash's fur, a soothingly repetitive motion. The softness, the familiar smell of him, was grounding, driving away the chill of her fear.

Dash's response was a deep, rumbling bark that resonated through the room, a symphony of pure joy. It echoed in the stillness, a melody of shared relief and happiness. "You're alive," she whispered, "And I can't explain how happy I am."

With a sigh of relief that seemed to drain her of her remaining energy, Jane made a hot pot of herbal tea, the aroma of which filled the space, attempting to soothe her rattled nerves. As she

sank into the welcoming softness of her couch, she wrapped her

fingers around the warm ceramic mug, the heat seeping into her

skin, a small comfort within the havoc.


Her contemplation was shattered by an abrupt knock from her

front door. Her heart skipped a beat, the sound ricocheting through

the quiet of her home, instantly igniting her nerves.

Thoughts of Officer Yolanda's stern countenance flashed

through her mind as she cautiously rose from the couch. She

padded silently across the wooden floor, her heartbeat pounding in

her ears.

She was met with an eerie emptiness when she passed through

the door's peephole. A chill ran down her spine as she stared into

the vacant space beyond her threshold. No one was there.

It could be a misguided prank or an innocent mistake. Yet as

she swiveled back towards the living room, her heart raced. A figure, hazy and shrouded in darkness, loomed pessimistically among her familiar furniture.

Rooted to the spot, Jane was a statue of petrified fear. An invisible force seemed to radiate from the figure. This penetrating gaze felt like it was burrowing into the deepest recesses of her psyche. A scream clawed at her throat, desperate for release. Still, her voice was a strangled whisper, soundless in the face of the inexplicable terror.

In the blink of an eye, the figure dissolved into the ether, leaving behind an empty room. Jane crumpled onto her couch, her body trembling as she gasped for breath. Was this a figment of her unraveling sanity? Was she teetering on the brink of madness?

A sense of urgency gnawed at her, realizing she needed to act. Yet, the path forward was shrouded in uncertainty. A rush of questions and fear churned within Jane's mind, a whirl of confusion and terror. She strained to rationalize the surreal events, but her thoughts were a jumbled puzzle, each piece more terrifying than the last. Amid the chaos, a singular belief took root - an imminent catastrophe loomed over her, a shadow she couldn't seem to escape.

She stayed cooped up for days in her home, too scared to leave. She couldn't speak to anyone, not even her closest friends or family.

The shadowy figure continued to haunt her, appearing in her dreams and even when she was awake. She felt like she was losing her grip on reality and didn't know how to stop it.

A wave of desperation washed over Jane, the chilling realization that her existence was flawed She mustered the courage to seek help anonymously on the internet. There, she stumbled upon a virtual sanctuary - a support group for individuals grappling with the aftermath of trauma.

Immersed in their shared narratives, Jane discovered a resemblance of understanding. Their stories were similar to her fears and doubts, their resilience lighting a spark of hope in the cavernous dark of her despair. She wasn't alone in her struggle;

others had traversed this path and emerged, not unscathed, but victorious.

"Is it real or just a figment of my imagination?" She often muttered, her eyes darting around, half-expecting the shadowy figure to materialize. It seemed to lurk in her peripheral vision, a sinister game of hide-and-seek that she was unwilling to participate in. This game was no child's play; it was a chilling dance with an unseen predator.

Windows were shrouded, and the door remained steadfastly bolted. The world outside became a forbidden territory she dared not venture into. Her fear bloomed into a monstrous entity as the weeks stretched into an unending nightmare. The figure, she was convinced, intended to harm her, its vindictive presence a constant shadow in her life.

The spectral figure began to infiltrate Jane's dreams in an eerie twist of events. It perched itself on the edge of her bed, its silhouette softened by the glow of her dream world. It spoke in a voice that was unexpectedly soothing, weaving tales of benign intentions and promises of aid.

Initially, Jane's skepticism reared its head. The entity that had been the source of her unending terror was now competing for her trust. Yet, the figure's relentless assurances slowly wore down her reservations, its persistence igniting a spark of belief within her.

That night, Jane was trapped in a terrifying state of sleep paralysis. It felt like she had been plunged into a timeless gorge, unable to distinguish between sleep and wakefulness.

Once a mere shadow, the figure stood at her bedroom door. Blinking, Jane found it had translocated to her bedside, the shadows merging into a tangible human form. Panic surged within her as she strained to move, her heart thudding violently.

Jane squeezed her eyes shut, her mind swirling in confusion. When she dared to open them again, her bedside was vacant. Jane scanned her room, the details eerily vivid in the murky gloom. Assembling her strength, she managed to roll onto her side, a shiver of cold slicing through her.

What she saw next froze her blood. An older woman lay on John's side of the bed, her gaze fixed on Jane. The words she whispered curled around Jane like tendrils of icy fear, "I found you, Jane. 'Hide and Seek' is my favorite game. Now we can play forever. Count to 10, and we play again, again, and again…."

The woman's face abruptly loomed into Jane's field of vision, a chilling smile playing on her lips. Once a calm brown, her eyes turned into a startling green, their glow piercing the darkness, leaving Jane in a rumbling terror.

With a jolt that felt like lightning surging through her veins, Jane shattered the chains of her sleep paralysis. She shot upright, her arms flailing through the air as if to fend off an unseen adversary. Roused from his slumber by her sudden movement, Dash skittered off the bed to seek refuge on the floor.

A cold terror gripped her as she slowly turned to face John's side of the bed, her heart pounding like a war drum against her chest. She braced herself for the monstrous aspect of the older woman, the remnants of her chilling words still lingering in the air.

But there was nothing. Just an expanse of new sheets, faintly illuminated by the ghostly moonlight seeping through the window. Jane's fingers tentatively explored the space, expecting to encounter the cold flesh of the woman. Yet all she found was the familiar fabric of her bedding, the area as empty as her relieved exhale.

She and Dash were alone in the room, the terrifying encounter reduced to a lingering fright that clung to the shadows. The room was once again her own, the spectral visitor a chilling memory imprinted on her mind.

After a few minutes, the room's silence was punctured by a haunting melody. It was the familiar tune of the music box, a device she had transferred to the living room as a decorative piece. Its notes stem from a much closer vicinity, weaving an eerie lullaby that prickled her skin.

Hesitantly, she reached for John's pillow, her fingers brushing against something solid. A cold wave of realization washed over her as she revealed the music box, fully wound up and nestled

181

under the pillow as though deliberately hidden. She timidly picked it up, her gaze fastened on the intricately carved chest as she grappled with the surreal turn of events.

With a shaky hand, she activated the flashlight on her phone, bathing the room in a condensed white light. Her heart pounded in her chest as a bizarre urge seized her, a burning need to uncover the origins of this mysterious item.

The room around her seemed to close in, the walls whispering secrets yet to be revealed. The music box in her hand felt heavier, its melody a sinister soundtrack to the unfolding mystery. The horror of the unknown was quickly replaced by a determination to uncover the truth, no matter how terrifying it might be.

Jane remained unaware of the sad tale that bound the spectral figure and the music box, an object of beauty she had acquired from an obscure antique shop. The music box was a masterpiece of craftsmanship, its wooden exterior adorned with elaborate carvings that danced under the light.

Once upon a time, this ornamental relic had been the prized possession of Amelia, a gifted musician whose talent was as insightful as the torment that shaded her life. The music box was her silent companion, a receptacle into which she poured her soul, each note a fragment of her joys and sorrows.

Amelia's life was a symphony woven with threads of suffering and loss. Each hardship was a sad note, a dark undertone that gave depth to the melody of her existence. The music box, thus, was more than a mere object.

It was a solid piece of Amelia's life, an enduring testament to her resilience in adversity. Despite the passage of time, Amelia's essence lingered, intertwined with the music box just as her fingers once partnered with the keys of her piano.

Years ago, Amelia had experienced a devastating tragedy, leaving her grief-stricken and isolated. Her sorrow manifested as dark energy slowly seeped into the music box she treasured dearly. Over time, the music box became a vessel for her pain, eventually giving birth to the shadowy figure that haunted Jane.

The spectral figure was a tangible echo of Amelia's torment, a phantasmal embodiment of her sorrow and a distressing cry for relief. It was drawn to Jane like a moth to a flame, recognizing the familiar strains of struggle and vulnerability in her. There was a desperate hope that in Jane's company, it could find a measure of comfort.

As Jane's encounters with the figure became increasingly frequent, she began to discern uncanny parallels between her life and Amelia's tragic tale. This newfound awareness kindled a sense of empathy within Jane.

The figure, once a representation of fear and terror, had morphed into a symbol of shared pain. It was no longer an evil entity but a kindred spirit tethered to her by the threads of shared suffering.

The haunting presence, once a source of dread, was now a testament to their shared human experience, a reminder that even in the face of despair, one is never alone.

With relentless determination, Jane plunged into Amelia's history, driven by an unwavering goal to liberate the figure from its perpetual torment. Her quest led her back to the antique shop, its musty scent heavy with secrets. She sought out the shopkeeper, hoping for revelations that would serve as keys to unlocking Amelia's mysterious past.

Jane's mission morphed into an enlightening journey, a voyage through the wild waves of Amelia's life and an untimely end. As she navigated this turbulent sea, Jane would uncover layers of her psyche, learning the transformative powers of healing, forgiveness, and redemption.

United by their shared ordeal, Jane and the figure would brave the storm, striving to shatter the constraints that bound them to their tormenting fear and pain.

Jane's pursuit of truth led her to a quaint town where Amelia's melancholy melodies once resonated through the cobbled streets. As she meandered through the city, Jane was gripped by an uncanny sense of déjà vu, as if retracing forgotten steps.

Here, she unearthed a core chapter of Amelia's life - a tale of forbidden love with a fellow musician named Thomas, whose abrupt disappearance cast shadows on Amelia's subsequent demise.

The town's inhabitants whispered tales of this lost love, a romantic saga marred by jealousy and betrayal. Jane's relentless digging unveiled a shocking reality - Amelia's premature death was no accident but the result of a crime of passion orchestrated by a green-eyed rival.

The chilling twist was that the rival was not a fellow human but an evil entity. This ancient spirit had been the town's spectral resident for centuries. This sinister force thrived on the townsfolks' agony and despair, its existence a chilling testament to their suffering.

Incensed by Amelia and Thomas' blossoming love, the entity possessed one of Amelia's confidantes, manipulating them into committing the heinous act before succumbing to their tragic end.

To help Amelia's spirit find peace and break the figure's chains, Jane must confront the evil spirit and uncover the truth about Thomas' disappearance. She enlisted the help of a local medium, who guided her through a séance to communicate with Amelia and Thomas' spirits.

The local medium, known as Madame Zara, is a woman of notable oddity. She's a petite, elderly woman with crimson hair styled in a voluminous beehive. Her eyes are a startling shade of violet, which she attributes to her spiritual sensitivity. She dresses in layers of colorful, mismatched scarves and chunky, exotic jewelry that clinks melodically whenever she moves.

Zara is known for her dramatic flair; she punctuates her speech with grand gestures and speaks in riddles, often leaving people more confused than enlightened. She has an eccentric habit of conversing with spirits even when no one else is around.

Despite her quirks, she has a kind heart and is committed to helping Jane. Her spirit animal, a chatty parrot named Oracle, accompanies her everywhere, often interrupting her readings with cryptic comments of its own.

Jane's decision to intercede was not simple, borne out of a desire to be a hero or a savior. A complex bouquet of emotions and motivations propelled her into this spectral conflict.

Her life was in chaos that mirrored the unrest that Amelia's spirit was experiencing. The thought of another soul trapped in a similar whirlwind of confusion and despair reiterated her internal struggle, and Jane felt an inexplicable pull toward helping Amelia.

She believed that if she could help Amelia find peace, she could find an impression of herself. She could untangle the knots in her life by resolving Amelia's unfinished business.

Moreover, the persistent presence of the mischievous figure in her life constantly reminded her of her vulnerability. The figure's presence reflected her fears and insecurities, amplifying them until they became unbearable. By helping Amelia, Jane hoped to banish the figure from her life to reclaim her sanctuary.

Jane cautiously stepped into Madame Zara's dimly lit store, the air heavy with the scent of incense. Her eyes scanned the room, taking in the array of mystical artifacts displayed on aged wooden shelves. The flickering candlelight cast eerie shadows on the cracked walls, adding an air of mystery to the space.

As Jane approached Madame Zara, the sound of a distant wind chime tinkling in the background reached her ears, mingling with the whispers of ancient spirits that seemed to echo through the room.

Jane looked at Madame Zara, her eyes filled with skepticism. "I found your name in an online forum. They said you were the best, but this... it's a lot to take in."

Madame Zara gave a melodramatic wave of her hand, bracelets jingling. "My dear, I've been conversing with the spirits longer than you've been alive. It's not a matter of belief but of perception."

"But why me? Why is this spirit, Amelia, contacting me?" Jane asked, frustration creeping into her voice.

Leaning back in her chair, Zara regarded Jane with her vibrant violet eyes. "You, Jane, are intuitive. More than you realize. Amelia sees that in you. She has a message, a truth that needs to be uncovered, and she trusts you to find it."

Oracle, perched on Zara's shoulder, squawked, "Trust! Trust!"

Jane sighed, running a hand through her hair. "Okay, I'll try. For Amelia and for Thomas."

Zara smiled, her eyes twinkling. "That's the spirit, my dear. Now, let's begin our journey into the unknown together."


As the séance progressed, the room grew colder, and the air was filled with eerie, uneasy energy. Zara summoned the spirits of Amelia and Thomas, and they revealed the truth: Thomas had been trapped by the evil spirit, forced to endure endless torment in a hidden realm between the living and the dead.

"We are dealing with a dark entity here. Oh yes…" Zara licked her lips and shook her arms to create a sense of urgency. "Oh I like this one. Filthy to say the least. You are one angry spirit! What could possibly make you so angry, my little demon?"

"Filthy! Filthy spirit!" Squawked Oracle.

"Pipe down, feather baby, I am trying to absorb all this…evil. Yes…" Zara's eyes rolled into the back of her head, and she started trembling erratically.

"Madame Zara… Are you ok?" Jane waved her hand in front of her face and snapped her fingers.

Madame Zara's eyes snapped open with unsettling intensity, and her voice emerged from the depths of darkness, sending chills down Jane's spine. "I have found you, Jane! Now, it is your turn to cower... Count to ten, for the game begins again!"

Jane's senses were overwhelmed by the ominous atmosphere that engulfed the room. The flickering candlelight cast grotesque shadows on the walls as if they were haunting specters lurking in the corners. Like ancient portals to the unknown, Zara's eyes held a mesmerizing and foreboding allure that ensnared Jane's soul.

With an unearthly resonance, Zara's voice echoed through the room, its haunting melody laced with a twisted sense of amusement. Jane felt a mixture of fascination and deep unease, as if she had stepped into a realm where reality and nightmare intertwined. The weight of Zara's words hung in the air, suffocating Jane with a sense of impending doom.

The room itself seemed to pulse with an unworldly energy, as though the very fabric of the universe strained under the weight of its secrets. Jane's heart pounded in her chest, each beat reverberating with anxiety, while her breath came in shallow gasps, struggling to keep pace with the racing thoughts in her mind.

Zara's sudden jerk in the chair startled Jane, snapping her back to reality. The medium's wide eyes, now free of the trance, sparkled with an almost mischievous glint. It was as if Zara had glimpsed into an ethereal realm and returned, intoxicated by the experience.

Jane couldn't help but feel a mixture of awe and anxiety as she awaited Zara's response. The room fell into an expectant silence, broken only by the distant howl of the wind outside.

With a flourish, Zara leaned forward, her voice excited. "Wow, mama really felt that one. Oh yeah…"

"Oh, my dear, the 'heart'… I caught sight of a heart, but it wasn't your typical kind. It was a peculiar encounter, something out of the ordinary. It piqued my curiosity, leading me to explore its depths further. It's fascinating how this spirit has become so obsessed with you."

Jane felt a chill that seemed to emanate from the very depths of her soul. The weight of the task ahead bore down upon her, a heavy burden she was determined to carry. She knew that to bring an end to this twisted game, she must venture into the heart of darkness.

"Well…I actually understand… it was talking about the heart of the woods" Jane replied, her voice tinged with both weariness and determination. "I will find the heart, and put an end to this insanity."

Madame Zara's face broke into a wide grin, her idiosyncrasy shining through. "Bravo, my dear! You have the spirit of a true adventurer. Remember, the spirits will await you if you ever need guidance on your journey."

With those final words, Zara's demeanor shifted, and she seemed to withdraw into herself, lost in her own mystical thoughts. The room returned to its hushed stillness, leaving Jane with a newfound sense of purpose and a burning desire to bring closure to this haunting ordeal.

Upon ensuring the well-being of Dash, Jane hastily made her way to her vehicle and embarked on a journey toward a destination she had previously investigated. The location in question was an abandoned residence, which she had gathered information about, and was approximately thirty minutes from the city center. An intuition stirred within her, indicating that this place held the key to the issue at hand.

To save Thomas and free Amelia's spirit, Jane had to confront the evil spirit and release Thomas from its clutches. With newfound knowledge and a determination to help her friend, Jane ventured down a dirt road through the woods where the heart was said to reside.

About a mile off the main road, Jane found an ancient, crumbling mansion – the lair of the evil spirit. As she entered the mansion, she felt the presence of the heart, its sinister energy weighing heavily on her. Jane bravely faced the apparition, using her understanding of Amelia's tragic story as a weapon against it.

As Jane mustered her courage, she stepped cautiously into the dilapidated house, its ancient floorboards groaning beneath her weight. The air was heavy with the scent of decay, mingling with the musty aroma of forgotten memories. Dust particles danced in the dim light that filtered through cracked windows, casting shadows on the peeling wallpaper.

The creaking broke the silence of a door swinging open ominously in the draft. Jane's heart raced, and her senses heightened with concern and determination. She could hear the faint whispers of the wind as it whispered through the broken glass as if the house itself was urging her to proceed.

In the heart of the house, Jane found herself in a dimly lit chamber, its walls adorned with faded tapestries that depicted scenes from a long-forgotten era. The air grew colder, sending a chill down her spine as if the very presence of the evil spirit permeated the room.

Suddenly, a voice, dripping with malice, filled the chamber. "I can't believe you are standing in front of me. Our souls can finally be together!" The spirit materialized before Jane, its form shrouded in darkness, its eyes burning with an otherworldly fire.

Jane steadied herself, her voice filled with a mixture of determination and compassion. "I have come to release Thomas from your clutches and bring peace to Amelia's spirit. I've played your little game, and I can't say it has been fun."

The spirit let out a hollow laugh, its voice echoing through the chamber. "Release them? Jane, you break my little heart. Thomas and I are nothing, it's not what it looks like!"

Undeterred, Jane met the spirit's gaze, her eyes ablaze with an inner fire. "What are you talking about? No, Thomas belongs to Amelia, and I belong to John. Love will always triumph over darkness or whatever you are."

The apparition withered back, its spectral form wavering like a candle in the wind. Through gritted ghostly teeth, it spat, "Your comprehension of love is laughable. You fail to grasp the potent ties that burden them to my essence."

"If you truly comprehend love, you would sense that John's flame has not yet been extinguished. Because here's the kicker, darling... he's not in here."

Jane's voice was firm, resonating with an ironclad belief. "What exactly are you implying about John?"

"In the spectral realm. I've kept my spot vacant for you and only you. Thomas holds no place in my spectral heart. You, Jane, are my destined partner."

"Then... he is still among the living!"

"Who, John? Well duh little goober. If you loved him you would know that."

"I... I have known that. My mind has always focused on the worst possible scenarios. Love transcends all boundaries, even those of life and death. Amelia's love for Thomas is a force that can never be extinguished – Same with John and I."

The room seemed to tremble, its walls pulsating with the struggle between light and darkness. Jane closed her eyes, channeling all her energy, and whispered a heartfelt plea. "Amelia, Thomas, hear my words. Your love is stronger than any darkness. It is time to break free and find strength in each other's arms."

"Jane, you make me out to be some kind of monster. I've lived inside you your whole life. I don't want you to suffer alone, we can suffer together... forever."

"You are confusing love with obsession. Love needs to be equal on both sides. John is my soulmate, not you or anyone else. Thomas and Amelia are soulmates, you are just pathetic."

"Jane, you upset me, I can't let Thomas go, as he is my only leverage to keep you in my little pocket."

"I'll make you a deal then. If John and I separate, then you can have me...forever. But you have to release Thomas and leave me alone."

"Intriguing. This would be a binding contract, no funny business. Oh Jane, you make me so happy again! You have a deal. I'll leave you alone, but I can't promise I won't be watching. Hehe."

As Jane opened her eyes, a blinding light erupted from within her, engulfing the spirit in a brilliance that defied the shadows. The spirit writhed in agony, its form dissipating into nothingness. It vanished with a final, desperate wail, leaving a sense of peace that permeated the chamber.

As the silence settled, Thomas's spirit emerged from the shadows, a smile of gratitude on his face. Amelia's spectral form materialized beside him, her essence shimmering with newfound serenity. Once held captive by the darkness, their love now radiated with a flash of undeniable brilliance.

Jane stood in awe, a witness to the power of love and the triumph of compassion. The air felt lighter, filled with a sense of hope and renewal. She had fulfilled her mission, bringing peace to the tormented spirits and dispelling the oppressive darkness that had plagued the town for far too long.

With a sigh of relief, Jane stepped back from the chamber, her heart filled with a profound sense of accomplishment. The house once shrouded in darkness, now seemed to exhale, its walls echoing a soft sigh of gratitude. Jane knew that her journey had left an indelible mark on her soul, forever intertwining her life with the mystical and the extraordinary.

As she stepped back into the world outside, the sunlight bathed her in warmth, a gentle breeze brushing against her skin. The fragrance of blooming flowers filled the air, a reminder that life continued to unfold, guided by the enduring power of love.

In the aftermath of her adventure, Jane's perception of John's fate shifted. A seed of hope sprouted amid the anguish of her loss, supported by the conviction that John was still among the living. The spectral figure had inadvertently been guiding her through the fog of uncertainty.

Inspired by her newfound determination, Jane stood on the threshold of another mystery - the mystery of John's disappearance. Amelia's tragic past and her confrontation with the figure had kindled a flame within her that would illuminate the path to the truth that lay shrouded in the shadows of the unknown. Her heart, once struggling, now pulsed with the rhythm of resolve, ready to unravel the chapters of her story.

Jane's journey was a challenging one. She had to face the evil entity head-on, which required immense courage. The entity did not reveal anything about John's whereabouts. However, she was determined more than ever to find him.

Throughout her journey, Jane learned a valuable lesson - that sometimes, helping others could lead to self-discovery and healing. Helping Amelia brought peace to the troubled spirit and helped Jane reconcile her fears and insecurities. It was a demonstration of the transformative power of compassion and empathy.

# PART 2

# 12

John, an ambitious investigative journalist with an insatiable thirst for truth, had stumbled upon a lead that promised to expose a hidden government conspiracy. Little did he know that his relentless pursuit of the truth would soon turn his world upside down.

The puzzle pieces fell into place as he delved deeper into his investigation. John pieced together fragments of information that painted a disturbing picture of corruption and deceit at the highest levels of power. The gravity of what he had uncovered weighed heavily on his conscience, but he knew he had a duty to bring the truth to light.

However, his tenacity had not gone unnoticed. Abernathy, a cunning and influential figure within the government organization at the center of the conspiracy, recognized the threat John posed. Determined to protect the secrets at all costs, Abernathy orchestrated a calculated plan to silence him.

It was a fateful day when John found himself ensnared in Abernathy's trap. Perhaps it was a tip-off that led him to a seemingly innocent meeting, or maybe he stumbled upon something he shouldn't have. The details were hazy, lost in the fog of uncertainty that shrouded his memory.

In the blink of an eye, John's world shattered. He awoke to find himself confined, imprisoned in a place that seemed to exist beyond the boundaries of the law. It was a secret detention center, a covert facility designed to hold those who knew too much, where the usual rules of justice held no sway.

Fear and confusion gripped John as he grappled with the reality of his situation. He felt the weight of Abernathy's control pressing down upon him, his every move scrutinized and manipulated. The walls seemed to close in, and the air grew heavy with the atmosphere of coercion.

As John searched for answers, he discovered that escape was futile. Abernathy had devised a cruel and effective method to ensure his compliance—an explosive collar. The collar was a constant reminder of the dire consequences that awaited any rebellion or attempt to expose the truth.

Days went on, and hope flickered like a dying flame. His knowledge consumed John's thoughts, the damning secrets that could change the course of history. He desired freedom, not only for himself but for the sake of all those who remained oblivious to the truth that had been hidden from them.

Within the confines of his imprisonment, John questioned his resilience. Would he be able to withstand the relentless pressure, the psychological torment inflicted upon him? The answers eluded him, but deep within his spirit, a flicker of determination burned bright. He knew that he had a responsibility to fight for justice, to expose the darkness that had ensnared him and countless others.

As John grappled with the unknown, the unfathomable figure of Abernathy loomed large in his thoughts. The man behind the conspiracy held the key to his imprisonment, and unraveling Abernathy's motives became an obsession.

But for now, John focused on survival, finding the strength to endure and bide his time, waiting for the opportunity to reclaim his freedom and expose the truth to the world.

In the depths of his confinement, John's thoughts often drifted to Jane, his beloved partner who had been left behind in a world oblivious to his predicament. Memories of their shared moments of laughter and love were inspirations of hope, providing comfort among the darkness surrounding him.

He longed for her presence, her warm embrace, and the reassuring touch of her hand. Jane's absence left an ache in his heart, a constant reminder of the life he had been forcefully separated from.

As the days stretched into weeks, John's desperation to return to Jane grew with each passing moment. He longed to hear her voice, to see her smile, and to share the burden of his captivity with her. But Abernathy's grip was unrelenting, and escape seemed like an elusive dream.

Within the confines of the secret detention center, John's appearance bore the weight of his ordeal. His once vibrant eyes, filled with determination and curiosity, now held a glimmer of melancholy. His face, imprinted with worry lines, spoke volumes of the mental and emotional toll he endured.

The absence of being able to go outside and the monotony of his surroundings had taken a toll on John's physical well-being. His once athletic frame had withered, resulting from limited movement and the constant stress of his confinement. Yet, despite the toll on his body, a fire burned within him—an unwavering resolve to hold onto his identity and the truth he carried.

Each passing day brought John closer to a grim realization— that his freedom was a distant memory, replaced by the cold steel bars and unyielding prison walls. The sense of entrapment weighed heavily on his soul, chipping away at his spirit. But even in the darkest of moments, he refused to surrender.

Imprisoned, John clung to the remnants of hope that lingered within his heart. His mind was a battleground, torn between the desire to protect himself and the burning need to expose the truth. Frustration mixed with determination as he meticulously planned his next move, searching for any crack in Abernathy's impenetrable fortress.

John's resolve hardened as the heavy iron door closed behind him, sealing him away from the world he once knew. He vowed to survive, to outlast the shadows that threatened to consume him. In the depths of his imprisonment, he strengthened himself against the despair, aware that his silence meant the endurance of Abernathy's malice.

John's determination grew more vigorous, fueled by his love for Jane, knowledge, and the undying hope that justice would ultimately prevail. Though imprisoned physically, his spirit remained unbroken, ready to face the challenges ahead and fight for the day when the truth would be set free.

Intrigued by John's steady determination, Abernathy discreetly approached Riverdale. He had heard whispers of John's exceptional skills and unwavering loyalty. and now, he saw an opportunity to recruit him for a venture that surpassed any ordinary profession.

Abernathy, with an air of calculated charisma, approached John, offering him a proposition that would forever change the course of his life. The job presented an unparalleled opportunity, promising not only a substantial increase in salary but a chance to delve into a world shrouded in mystery and intrigue. The catch, however, was a double-edged sword with the potential for both great reward and unfathomable consequences.

Within the confines of the facility, information was treated as the most precious commodity, locked away in secure files and guarded by an impenetrable fortress of caution. Conversations were stripped of any trace of detail, veiled in secrecy to protect the delicate balance maintained within the concealed operations. It was a world where trust was forged in the crucible of silence, where the boundaries of loyalty were tested at every turn.

For John, this offer was a siren's call, beckoning him towards a path that promised fulfillment and prosperity beyond his wildest dreams. It was an opportunity that not only held the potential to elevate his own life but that of his beloved Jane as well.

The magnitude of this offer weighed heavily upon John's conscience, a decision that would reverberate through the corridors of their future.

As Abernathy presented this tantalizing offer, the gravity of the situation settled upon John's shoulders, the weight of his decision deep in the air. This was a pivotal moment, a crossroads where the paths of ordinary existence and extraordinary potential converged. The allure of the unknown beckoned, its promises intertwined with a web of uncertainty. All John had to do was wait for a recruiter to approach him with the details.

From Jane's perspective, she understood that he was working on a government project as a journalist that needed time underground and the use of heavy machinery and sophisticated technology.

An excavation project needed hours and hours of work. When he came home, he had to work on analyzing the findings in a room with strict deadlines.

The fear of losing his job and the havoc it would cause in his lively hood with Jane kept him going. John started to read journal entries of other workers that claimed to have experienced this groundbreaking, state-of-the-art A.I. technology.

John read about someone buying a car in the early 1940s, J.F.K. getting shot from only several feet away, or watching the space shuttle explode in person. It was described as a super realistic experience that places you in a time you would never have experienced.

John remained skeptical as he only spoke to people who saw these events, and for all he knew, it was fiction in a storybook. His inquisitiveness strengthened, and he volunteered for one of these experiments.

A week after showing interest, he received a large packet labeled "Highly Confidential." It was a multipage contract about an inch thick, requiring initials on every page and a final signature on the last page.

John read the first few pages, which seemed more like a marketing technique to try out a "once in a lifetime" opportunity. He skimmed through the fine print, placed the packet in the return envelope, and dropped it in the nearest mailbox.

About a week later, John was waiting in line at his favorite coffee shop on his way to work. While waiting, he was approached by a stranger dressed in all black. The stranger appeared to be in their thirties, bald, and had an impressively twirled mustache that extended past their nostrils.

The stranger introduced themselves as a member of the SPITE project and requested that the individual accompany them. Without much choice, the individual followed the stranger through a closed door.

John's heart raced as he stood at the crossroads of uncertainty. The mysterious man, who exuded an air of intrigue and mystery, beckoned him with a subtle gesture. For a brief moment, John hesitated, his mind wrestling with the unknown risks that lay ahead. Yet, a surge of unyielding curiosity coursed through his veins, overpowering his doubts.

Taking a deep breath, John carefully surveyed his surroundings, his eyes darting from one detail to another. Satisfied with his assessment, he discreetly adjusted the buttons on his coat, ensuring every fastening was secured. This small act served as a metaphorical armor, a symbol of his determination to embark on this covert adventure.

With steady resolve, John followed in the wake of the distinguished gentleman, their footsteps echoing softly against the polished floors. The corridors, bathed in a dim, ethereal glow, seemed to whisper secrets of their own, heightening the suspense that hung in the air.

Each step forward brought John closer to the face of the unknown, his anticipation mingling with a tinge of unease.

Finally, the duo reached their destination, a heavy metal door that stood as an impenetrable barrier to the mysteries that lay beyond. The man effortlessly retrieved a key card from the depths of his pocket, its sleek surface reflecting the faint light. With a swift motion, he glided the card across the access panel, causing a satisfying click to resonate through the corridor.

As the door swung open, revealing a hidden world within, John's eyes widened in awe and intrigue. Before him lay a small, windowless room, immersed with an otherworldly glow stemming from an array of high-tech equipment. The room hummed with a symphony of soft beeps and whirrs, its purpose shrouded in secrecy.

In that moment, John's tenacity melded with the puzzling atmosphere of the room. He stepped forward, crossing the threshold, and a sense of destiny cloaked him. Together with the mysterious man, they embarked on a journey that would test their mettle and unravel the veils of the unknown.

"Welcome to the experiment," his voice cold and emotionless. "I am Riverdale, and I will oversee your participation in this groundbreaking project. Please, have a seat."

John cautiously sat in the middle of the room, his heart pounding. Riverdale handed him a pair of goggles and a set of headphones, instructing him to put them on.

"Once you're ready, I'll activate the system," Riverdale said, his fingers hovering over a series of buttons and switches. "You'll be transported, virtually, to a moment in history. Your task is to observe and report back on your experience. Remember, you are only an observer – you cannot interact or change anything."

John nodded, his curiosity piqued by the prospect of witnessing history firsthand. He put on the goggles and headphones, and his vision and hearing were immediately obscured.

Riverdale activated the system, and John felt a sudden jolt as his surroundings changed. He found himself standing on a crowded street, surrounded by people dressed in mid-20th-century attire. The air was filled with excitement, and as he looked around, he realized he was in Dallas on November 22, 1963 – the day of J.F.K.'s assassination.

John's heart raced as he took in the scene, knowing he was about to witness a pivotal historical moment. He watched from the sidelines as the presidential motorcade approached, J.F.K. smiling and waving at the cheering crowd. In the distance, he noticed a man lurking in the shadows, his expression sinister and his eyes locked on the president.

The crowd screamed as the gunshot rang out, and John instinctively ducked for cover. He knew he couldn't change the outcome, but the overwhelming sense of helplessness weighed heavily on him.

When the simulation ended, John found himself back in the small room with Riverdale, his body shaking from the intensity of the experience. He struggled to process what he had just witnessed, unable to shake the vivid images from his mind.

"You now understand the power of our technology," a hint of satisfaction in his voice. "But with this power comes accountability. We must use it wisely."

As John left the experiment room, a new sense of purpose emerged. He knew he couldn't ignore the potential consequences of such technology, and he became determined to uncover the true intentions behind the project. Little did he know, he was about to be drawn into a web of secrecy and danger, with his life in the balance.

A man named Riverdale, a figure of authority and influence, escorted him out, his actions dictating the trajectory of his life permanently. Riverdale was one of the founding fathers of the technology known as SPITE, a man whose fascination with computer science was as vast as the digital landscapes he explored.

Riverdale was a product of humble beginnings, raised in the confines of a small town, nestled in the comforting grip of a loving family. His upbringing was a needlepoint of common threads, yet this simplicity developed his extraordinary curiosity.

As a child, Riverdale was a container of endless questions, his curious mind constantly seeking to unravel the mysteries of the world that surrounded him. His fascination was particularly drawn to the mesmerizing world of computers and technology, where logic met creativity in a dazzling dance of possibilities.

As John sat across from Riverdale, the founder of SPITE, he couldn't help but feel a mix of awe and curiosity. The opportunity to delve into Riverdale's life story was too enticing to pass up. Leaning forward, John posed his question, "So, Riverdale, you're one of the founders of SPITE. How did you first become involved in technology?"

Riverdale's eyes lit up with a nostalgic gleam as he reminisced about his early years. "Yes, I've always been fascinated by technology, even from a young age," he replied. "Countless hours were spent hunched over the glowing screens of computers, my fingers dancing over the keys as I delved into the intricate workings of software and hardware. The digital world became my playground, and my thirst for knowledge grew stronger with each discovery."

Intrigued, John continued, "It sounds like your passion for technology led you to pursue higher education. What was your journey like in college?"

Riverdale nodded, a smile tugging at the corners of his lips. "Exactly. I heeded the calling and enrolled in a prestigious university renowned for its computer science program. Those years were transformative for me. I immersed myself in the intricate network of code and algorithms, and my natural aptitude shone through. I excelled, consistently etching my name at the top of the class roster."

Curiosity piqued, John asked, "After graduation, what kind of opportunities came your way?"

Riverdale's expression turned earnest. "My formidable skills did not go unnoticed," he replied. "A prominent tech company, a titan in technological innovation, swiftly recruited me. They entrusted me with a project of astronomical significance—the development of artificial intelligence. It was a thrilling challenge, and I poured my soul into it. Lines of code and complex equations consumed my every waking moment."

John couldn't help but be captivated by Riverdale's passion. "And what happened once the A.I. was finally created? Did you achieve what you had envisioned?"

Riverdale's eyes shimmered with pride and ambition. "The birth of the A.I. was a moment of triumph. Its capabilities surpassed even my ambitious expectations. But you know, I couldn't rest on my achievements. My mind was already envisioning the potential for further enhancement. The journey had only just begun, and the possibilities were limitless."

As their conversation unfolded, John drew deeper into Riverdale's world, his thirst for knowledge mirrored in the founder's unwavering pursuit of technological advancement. Riverdale's rise intertwined with John's quest for truth, revealing a complex web of motivation and ambition that would shape their paths unexpectedly.

As John continued to listen intently to Riverdale's story, Abernathy was mentioned for the first time. He couldn't help but sense that Riverdale was not a fan. "Riverdale, what happened when Abernathy set his sights on your groundbreaking A.I.?"

Riverdale's expression grew somber; his voice tinged with a hint of regret. "Abernathy, a titan in the tech industry known for his ruthless strategies, caught wind of the transformative potential held by my A.I. He was captivated, convinced that it could redefine the contours of the tech landscape. With scant regard for moral boundaries, he was determined to acquire it."

John's curiosity deepened, and he queried, "How did you navigate the predatory gaze of Abernathy? It must have been a challenging and perilous situation."

A flicker of determination sparked in Riverdale's eyes. "Indeed, it was a wild time," he replied. "But I refused to let Abernathy's predatory tactics dismantle everything I had worked for. I understood the immense responsibility that came with this groundbreaking technology. Abernathy and I came to an agreement, and we have worked together since. Actually, you will be reporting to him during the simulations."

Riverdale's voice resonated with a quiet resolve as he continued, "With the unwavering support of my team, we fortified our defenses and protected our creation. We implemented stringent security measures, safeguarding the A.I. from falling into the wrong hands. It was a constant battle, but we remained steadfast."

John couldn't help but be inspired by Riverdale's resilience and integrity. "Riverdale, how did you stay grounded and true to your principles during this struggle?"

A wistful smile graced Riverdale's face. "My humble beginnings served as an anchor," he replied. "I never forgot where I came from, the support and affection of my family and friends.

They reminded me of the importance of using my skills for the betterment of humanity."

He continued, "My passion guided me through the storm, ensuring that my pioneering work was always wielded as a force for good. I remained driven by the belief that technology could be a powerful instrument against injustice, inequality, and poverty."

John's admiration for Riverdale deepened as he realized the A.I.'s profound impact on the world. "Riverdale, it's incredible to hear how your creation transformed lives and brought hope to countless people. Can you share some examples of the A.I.'s impact?"

A warm glow appeared in Riverdale's eyes. "Certainly," he replied. "The A.I. extended a helping hand to the oppressed, offering opportunities for growth and empowerment. It played a pivotal role in transforming lives, painting hope across the canvas of the world. Through its abilities of independent thought, learning, and interaction, it reshaped the way we approached challenges, opening new doors for innovation and progress."

John was moved by Riverdale's vision and the impact he had made. The story of Riverdale's journey, and his unwavering dedication to using technology for the greater good, resonated deeply within John's quest for truth and justice. It fueled his determination to uncover the truth behind the conspiracy and ensure that the power of technology would be harnessed responsibly.

At first, Riverdale needed clarification about working with Abernathy's team due to a clash in values. However, Abernathy was an experienced negotiator who convinced Riverdale that his innovative A.I. system would be used for the greater good. Thus, with some hesitation, Riverdale decided to partner with them.

As the project unfolded, Riverdale's unease grew. His A.I., intended to signal hope, was being manipulated into a formidable weapon, the SPITE. It had the potential to wreak havoc on innocent lives. Riverdale was horrified at the monstrous creation his innovation had birthed and knew he had to intervene.

After Riverdale shared his story with John and led him out of the room, some time passed. Riverdale had already lost control of his creation, the A.I., before John's encounter with him. His protests against Abernathy's actions had been disregarded, and the SPITE had already been shaped according to Abernathy's intentions.

Abernathy remained unswayed by Riverdale's pleas, and it became clear to Riverdale that his groundbreaking work had been appropriated for malicious purposes.

Riverdale's journey was a brutal reminder of the dangers of misusing technology. He had learned the bitter truth that even the most compassionate innovations could be twisted into instruments of harm. Yet, he remained steadfast in his mission to ensure his A.I. would serve the way he intended. He soldiered on, undeterred by setbacks, and never lost sight of his vision for a better world.

As he grappled with the exploitation of his A.I., Riverdale knew he could not remain a passive observer. He needed a strategy and allies. His search led him to like-minded individuals willing to join him in intercepting Abernathy's sinister plans.

In his quest, Riverdale encountered The Sentinels, a group of proficient hackers and activists committed to unmasking corruption in the tech industry and combating the abuse of technology. He approached them, hopeful that they would align with his cause.

Initially, The Sentinels questioned Riverdale's motives. However, they pledged their support as they familiarized themselves with his narrative and unwavering commitment to ensuring his A.I. was used positively. This unlikely alliance was bound by their shared mission to halt Abernathy's SPITE weapon.

As they strategized together, Riverdale found himself forming bonds with The Sentinels. He grew particularly close to their leader, Cassidy, a gifted hacker with a solid moral compass. Their relationship deepened into mutual trust, and they shared their aspirations for a brighter future.

Just as they were on the brink of infiltrating Abernathy's empire and exposing his shady intentions, their plans crumbled. Abernathy, ever the cunning opponent, had somehow learned of their alliance. He used his immense resources to dismantle The Sentinels, silencing them individually.

Riverdale was shattered. The allies he had grown to trust were abruptly taken from him. The burden of stopping Abernathy and his SPITE weapon felt heavier than ever.

With The Sentinels neutralized, Abernathy's reign seemed invincible. His arrogance swelled, and he pursued power with renewed ruthlessness. As Riverdale watched from the shadows, he knew he had to find another way to disrupt Abernathy's plans. The stakes were escalating, and time was slipping away.

In a last-ditch effort, Riverdale decided to penetrate Abernathy's company alone. Despite the enormous risks and the likelihood of walking into a trap, he felt compelled to act. He could not stand by while Abernathy wreaked havoc with his A.I.

Riverdale entered Abernathy's inner circle using his intricate knowledge of the company and the intelligence gathered with The Sentinels. As an ambitious engineer eager to work at the forefront of technology, he searched for a way to sabotage the SPITE weapon.

But as Riverdale delved deeper into the company, he unearthed a shocking secret that altered his perception of Abernathy and the A.I. This revelation changed his mission's trajectory and forced him to question everything he was fighting for.

Undisclosed to Riverdale, Abernathy had been orchestrating a secret plan all along. Their collaboration served merely as a clever ruse, a smokescreen designed to divert Riverdale's attention. While Riverdale believed they were working towards a collective goal, Abernathy covertly fine-tuned the SPITE.

In the secret recesses of his company, disguised as Riverdale's study, Abernathy was edging closer to his ultimate purpose. He was on the brink of wielding a power that could alter the course of history. At the same time, Riverdale remained blissfully oblivious to his devious schemes.

# 13

As the first rays of dawn filtered through the window, John jolted from sleep by the rasping voice of Abernathy resonating through his room. His mentor's deep, piercing tones felt like a sledgehammer against the fragile silence, shattering the soft shell of his slumber.

John's eyes flickered open, heavy with the remnants of dreams and the weight of another day. His gaze, blurred and unfocused, fell upon the merciless hands of the clock. It was an all too familiar and unwelcome sight, the same harsh digits he had been forced to behold for what felt like an eternity.

Across the room, Abernathy's stern face was engraved with lines of chronic disapproval. His head moved in a slow, deliberate shake, the corners of his mouth turning downwards in a scowl of frustration. The room seemed to shrink under the gravity of his disappointment.

"Do you ever plan on being prepared?" Abernathy barked, each word peppered with a trace of boiling impatience.

"Get up, get dressed, and meet me in the same room, same time, wearing the same clothes as always!" he commanded, his words forming a rhythmic mantra of monotony and discipline. His tone was as steadfast as the routine he was reinforcing, a constant reminder of the repetitive, unchanging life John was leading.

John lifted his hand in a lazy salute, his eyes twinkling with a hint of rebellious amusement that contradicted the moment's seriousness. He then slipped into his vibrant red jumpsuit, the bold color conflicting with the dreary surroundings. It clung to him like a second skin, the fabric whispering secrets of extraordinary adventures.

Next, he settled his special glasses onto the bridge of his nose. The lenses are tinted with a futuristic sheen. He slipped his feet into cushioned slippers, their soft embrace a small comfort against the harsh realities of his situation. He then reached for his journal, a faithful confidante in his solitary journey, its worn pages filled with a script that danced between hope and despair.

After a cursory self-inspection in the mirror, his reflection staring back at him with stoic resolve, he exited his room. The long corridor outside stretched out before him like an endless tunnel, the dullness of the grey walls broken only by the doors that punctuated them. He navigated its length to the second door on the left, a path he had tread countless times before.

The unyielding white paint that blanketed the walls, the imposing metal doors, and the sparsely furnished space were simple reminders of his restricted liberty. The room was a prison in all but name, devoid of the warmth of personal touches.

Yet, he understood his purpose, the reason for his self-imposed incarceration. The room's centerpiece, the SPITE machine, stood in quiet dominance. An acronym for Subjective Protocol Interface Terminal and Efficacy, the beacon lit his path to freedom.

Despite the dreary setting, the machine promised liberation, and this promise held John captive in this sterile, monochromatic world.

Abernathy's imposing figure entered, confident strides of his authority as he navigated the sterile room. John had already nestled himself into the SPITE, the machine's cold, metallic demeanor contrasting with his warm vitality. Around his neck, he wore a sensitive collar, a sleek band of technology that held a deadly secret. It was rigged to trigger an explosion if he strayed beyond its set proximity for more than thirty seconds - a chilling deterrent to any thoughts of escape.

John had never mustered the audacity to verify the collar's destructive capabilities. He muttered to himself, his voice barely a whisper in the silent room, "Is it worth experimenting with? Probably not."

It was a rhetorical question, the answer already fixed in his mind with clarity. The risk was too significant.

Abernathy was a riddle that evoked fear and respect among those who crossed his path. Despite his erratic behavior that bordered on insanity, he had a pleasant demeanor that could disarm even the most guarded individuals.

His intelligence was intimidating, and his power held a menacing promise of unbounded potential. There was no task too daunting, no obstacle too formidable for him to overcome.

Abernathy's ability to find comfort in sleep was most unsettling, even when his actions led to the loss of lives and the shattering of families. His conscience, it seemed, was immune to the haunting guilt that would plague most. His capacity for detachment was as chilling as it was impressive, painting a picture of a man who was as complex as he was formidable.

Abernathy's gaze, as cold and hard as ice, swept over the room, landing disrespectfully on the imprisoned individuals. His lips curled into a sneer, an expression of despise and superiority. His reputation as a ruthless oppressor was well-known and well-earned, and he rejoiced in the terror he inspired.

He derived a perverse satisfaction from the fear of his captives, their desperation a glaring counterpoint to his unrelenting authority. The thrill of asserting his dominance, the rush of adrenaline when he inflicted pain upon those who dared to cross him, was a willful pleasure he eagerly indulged in.

Before he assumed his role at the grim facility, Abernathy's character was already cast in this cold-blooded mold. With a childhood marred by hardships and emotional havoc, he quickly learned that cruelty and an unforgiving nature were the keys to survival. This perspective, born out of necessity, had clung to him like a silhouette throughout his life.

As he ascended the ranks at the facility, this harsh mentality only amplified. His rise to power fortified his belief in his survival philosophy. It provided an environment that allowed his cruel tendencies to flourish unrestricted. Abernathy was a product of his past and a testament to the power of circumstances in shaping a man's character.

Despite his outward confidence, however, Abernathy was deeply insecure. He was afraid of losing his power and position, and he constantly looked over his shoulder, fearing that someone would try to take him down. This fear had made him even more cruel and oppressive as he sought to stamp out any potential threats to his authority.

As John observed Abernathy prowling the room, interacting with the other prisoners, a cocktail of disgust and hatred gnawed at his insides. Abernathy was a human embodiment of malice, a specter that haunted their lives.

With clarity as sharp as a blade, he understood that he had to devise a strategy to halt this beast before the sands of time ran out. Yet, he was painfully aware of the staggering challenge that lay ahead.

Abernathy leaned towards one of the prisoners in his chilling demeanor, his lips curling into a sinister grin. His voice slithered through the room, cold and remorseless, "You see, gentlemen, pain is a potent teacher. It sharpens the mind, don't you agree? And fear... fear is the greatest motivator of all. It's a fascinating dance, wouldn't you say?"

His words, devoid of empathy, echoed through the room, turning the air colder. John's resolve hardened; he would not let this monster reign unchecked.

Despite the formidable odds stacked against him, John was committed to dismantling Abernathy's reign of terror and bringing him to the harsh light of justice. He was acutely aware that the path before him was burdened with obstacles as winding as a mountain trail. Yet, his determination was as unyielding as the most intricate diamond.

He understood that the journey to topple Abernathy would require more than just courage; it would demand every ounce of his strength, every sliver of his cunning, and an unwavering commitment to his cause. The road ahead was long, potentially filled with setbacks and heartbreaks, but John was prepared to traverse the tumultuous terrain.

His resolve was fueled by a singular aim - to create a world where Abernathy could no longer inflict harm with his twisted games. The thought of a future free from Abernathy's tyranny was a beacon that guided him, a vision powerful enough to keep his spirit unbroken in the face of adversity. No matter the cost or sacrifices, John was ready to do whatever it took to turn this vision into reality.

Abernathy was an ex-NFL lineman, a burly behemoth who had once graced the line-up of the illustrious Dallas Cowboys. His tenure, however, was abruptly terminated when the league stumbled upon his unsavory record of public lewdness and animal cruelty.

The mystery of how such heinous details had slipped through the cracks during his signing still hung in the air, an unanswered question that cast a shadow over his short-lived career. Despite spending much time warming the benches, Abernathy had basked in the glory of a Super Bowl victory with his team. This achievement would forever remain tarnished by his subsequent actions.

Abernathy's tale involving a drunken camping escapade with his jock friends had been stamped into the archives of infamy. Spurred on by his comrades, a heavily intoxicated Abernathy had stripped to nothing more than his protective cup, setting off on a mission to trap a wild creature. When he failed to return after an hour, his worried friends sought help at a ranger station a few miles east.

On reaching the station, they were greeted by a bizarre sight - Abernathy, unconscious in the back seat of a patrol car, its lights casting a menacing red-and-blue glow. The presence of the boys startled the on-duty officer, prompting him to reach for his firearm instinctively. However, he stopped short of drawing it. "Can I help you, boys?" His query was laced with a touch of sarcasm.

"That's our friend in the back of your car. Is he okay? What happened?" a concerned voice from the group asked.

The officer's face morphed into a smirk, "Looks like your little buddy here got himself arrested for breaking the law. I can smell trouble all over you, boys. Care to explain why he's out here, flaunting his birthday suit?"

"We were playing a game, officer... and he must've wandered off. What is he being charged with?"

The officer's smirk widened, "A game that involves stripping in front of your pals? I can't say I'm keen on the details. Your friend is up for indecent exposure and assaulting an endangered animal. I caught him red-handed, wrestling a Whooping Crane. Meddling with endangered species is a federal crime, boys. We don't take it lightly. We're also investigating if this was done for... ahem... sexual pleasure. So, does your friend have a taste for frolicking with wildlife? Does he enjoy tickling the feathers of a forest bride, perhaps?"

The revelation left Abernathy's companions rooted to the spot, their faces drained of color. A heavy silence hung in the air before they abruptly spun on their heels and dashed away, their camaraderie evaporating in front of impending trouble. They left Abernathy to the mercy of the officer's probing questions and damning accusations.

Abernathy was now alone, grappling with the reality of his predicament. As he attempted to articulate a defense, he could feel the quicksand of his situation dragging him deeper into trouble. He reflected on the twisted path that had led him to this disastrous moment, his mind spinning with the uncertainty of what lay ahead.

Within a few years, two of the five boys on that fateful night succumbed to drug overdoses. Abernathy, however, would always recount the incident with disturbing humor, devoted to his belief that those boys had met their fate. Yet, a dark cloud of suspicion loomed over these tragic events: had Abernathy played a part in their untimely deaths?

John had posed this question to Abernathy the first time he'd heard the story. Abernathy's response had been chillingly sadistic. He'd claimed that the power to determine life and death should not rest in mortal hands.

"Death should be natural, but sometimes cause and effect can play a huge role," Abernathy had said. As he voiced these words, he'd raised his fists, one representing the cause, the other the effect, in a chilling demonstration of his twisted thinking.

A wave of distaste washed over John as Abernathy narrated his morbid tale, the casual recounting of the boys' demise leaving a bitter taste in his mouth. He was acutely aware of Abernathy's capacity for destruction. He couldn't help but wonder about the countless lives this man had shattered over the years.

"You're a sick man, Abernathy," John spat out, his voice heavy with disgust. His head shook in disbelief, his eyes hardening into icy shards. "How do you rationalize what you did to those boys? They were just children in the grand scheme of things."

Abernathy's response was a chilling laugh, a sound devoid of warmth. It echoed off the bare walls, a cruel symphony that made John's skin crawl. "Just children?" Abernathy echoed, his voice dripping with scorn. "They were weak, John. Incapable of handling the power I bestowed upon them. Their demise was inevitable, one way or another."

John stared at Abernathy, his eyes blazing with righteous fury. His fists clenched at his sides, knuckles white under the strain. "You're a monster, Abernathy. You've left a trail of devastation in your wake. How do you sleep at night, knowing the extent of the damage you've inflicted?"

Abernathy shrugged, his expression indifferent. "I do what I have to do to survive, John. You should know that better than anyone. We all have our demons and must sacrifice to keep them at bay."

John shook his head, unable to comprehend Abernathy's twisted logic. "I'll never understand you, Abernathy. You're a lost cause."

Abernathy just laughed again, his eyes glinting with amusement. "You're the lost cause, John. You'll never be able to stop me. I'm too powerful, too smart, too ruthless."

The organization had given John the title of a 'Subjector,' but he was far from your run-of-the-mill specimen. Subjectors were a rare breed with the unique ability to operate the machine. But John stood apart even in this scarce group - he was the only living manipulator in a lineage that spanned decades.

Over the years, only a handful of these exceptional individuals had emerged, their potential cut short by their premature deaths. It was whispered among the ranks that excessive use of the machine induced an addiction like the debilitating clutches of meth or heroin.

The withdrawal was a nightmarish ordeal, marked by severe side effects - delusions, violent mood swings, and at its most lethal, death itself.

John, however, was an anomaly. He could endure hours, even days, trapped within the machine's grasp without exhibiting the slightest sign of withdrawal. His resilience was a mystery, one that the organization was eager to unravel.

His captivity was not just about containment but about studying this extraordinary phenomenon. The odds of discovering another specimen with such a unique capability were minuscule, wobbling on the edge of impossibility. John was a living, breathing puzzle, and the organization was determined to solve him.

Abernathy's voice thundered through the room, his words disrupting the heavy silence as he paced restlessly around the space where John was situated.

"Not only can you bask in the marvel of the Subjective Protocol, but you can also shape the minds of those you observe," he exclaimed, a manic energy radiating from him. His gaze focused heavily on John's, a twisted grin on his lips. "So, what does that make you - a modern-day Moses or the Pied Piper of Hamelin?"

The secret to this manipulation lay in synchronizing brain wave frequencies with the Subjector. Yet, over the many years of experimentation, no one had managed to sustain this manipulation for more than a few fleeting seconds without spiraling into madness.

Legends of past Subjectors were crammed with horrific accounts of violent convulsions that spawned bone fractures, severed limbs, and, in some chilling instances, self-inflicted skin flaying.

Abernathy continued his tirade, his voice a chilling soundtrack to the gruesome stories he was recounting.

"I remember a young Subjector who castrated himself in a fit of madness, flinging his testicles around like a monkey hurling its feces."

Abernathy's laughter resonated through the room, a gruesome addition to his words.

"Pulled them off, just as you would yank a carrot from the ground. The janitor's face was a sight to behold when he was tasked with cleaning up the remains. Do you comprehend what this means, Johnny boy?" he queried with unsettling enthusiasm.

As Abernathy's words hung in the air, John's gaze hardened, locking onto Abernathy's gleeful eyes. Abernathy leaned in, dropping his voice to a conspiratorial whisper, a devilish spark in his eyes.

"Imagine the possibilities, John. What if we could travel back in time and impart a few ingenious tips to Ben Franklin to make his inventions a little more titillating? We could transform him into the pioneer of sex robot technology!"

His words, despite their wild nature, carried a connotation of dangerous ambition, a glimpse into the twisted vision Abernathy harbored.

John's eyebrows shot up in surprise. "What? Abernathy, that's wild. We can't just manipulate history like that."

Abernathy cackled, a mischievous sparkle dancing in his sapphire eyes.

"Aw, lighten up, John," he coaxed, mischief lacing his voice. "Just imagine the vast potential. We could amass unimaginable wealth, and it's not just about us. Consider the countless lives we could transform with our enhancements. Of course, these are only simulations of the past.

However, Riverdale believes you could put your thoughts and decisions into someone's mind like a freakin conscience. You know that little voice in your head deciphering right from wrong? Could you imagine what we could do with that power?"

John, however, shook his head, a wave of hate sweeping over him like a chilling wind.

His face twisted sternly as he responded, "I can't align myself with your plans, Abernathy. What you're proposing is morally reprehensible. We have no right to meddle with the fabric of history or puppeteer the thoughts and actions of unsuspecting individuals."

Abernathy scowled, his face turning red with anger. "You're weak, John. You don't have the stomach for this kind of work. You'll never be able to reach your full potential if your morals always hold you back. Man, I can't believe this crap I must put up with. You are lucky we have to keep you alive. Oh boy, I cannot wait until you start failing the simulations so we can spend more… quality time together."

John faintly leaned forward, a cunning smile pulling at the edges of his lips, his eyes dancing with an untold secret.

"It's my ethics that maintain my humanity, Abernathy," he stated, his voice laced with a subtle hint of condescension.

"But by all means, take your liberty if you wish to bear the burden of morphing Benjamin Franklin into the architect of lewd automatons. Just don't anticipate me lingering in the chaotic aftermath."

With that declaration, John reclined into the comforting embrace of his chair, his gaze unwaveringly fixed on Abernathy. He watched with thinly indirect amusement as Abernathy's face knotted into an expression of disapproval, his smugness barely hidden.

John was aware that he had outwitted Abernathy and felt satisfied with making the ethical choice.

He realized the quest for power and control was trivial in the grand scheme of things. What mattered were virtues like compassion, empathy, and love. These sentiments enriched life and made it an experience worth cherishing.

Abernathy's laughter echoed through the room, his eyes, greedy and glinting, beginning to glisten with crocodile tears. He thought John had yet to grasp the depth of the rabbit hole he'd fallen into.

Abernathy sank back into his chair, his eyes flickering with an uncontained thrill. "You hold the potential to bestow knowledge, my abnormal protégé," he exclaimed, the corners of his mouth curving into a sarcastic smile.

"Step aside, Google and Amazon, for our Johnny is here to claim his dominion. Google Earth, albeit impressive, is artificial, and Amazon, despite its merits, can't reshape the past to alter the future. Or something along those lines."

A rich chuckle resonated from John, a grin slowly spreading across his face, breaking his severe facade. "I understand your perspective, Abernathy," he confessed, his voice hinting amusement.

"And I won't deny, the prospect of utilizing our abilities to prevent wrongdoings and enhance the world is tempting. However, we must tread with caution. Without their consent, we can't thoughtlessly manipulate people's thoughts and actions."

Abernathy waved a dismissive hand. "Oh, come on, Johnny boy. We're not going to hurt anyone. We're just going to stop them from hurting others. Can you imagine stopping someone from committing a violent crime before they even do it? Think of the lives we could save and the families we could spare from heartbreak and tragedy."

John nodded slowly, his eyes fixed on Abernathy. "I know. And I want to help. But we have to be responsible for it. We must ensure we're not overstepping our boundaries or causing unintended consequences."

"I'm not referring to arbitrary homicides or those fantastical scenarios you glimpsed in 'Minority Report.' Have you seen that film featuring Tom Cruise and a cast of other actors who seem to fade into oblivion? Hello? Anyone in there?" Abernathy quipped, rapping his knuckles insistently against John's forehead, echoing in the silence.

John interjected abruptly, his voice laced with a hint of irritation, "Yes, I have seen that movie." His wish was for this unnerving conversation to reach its conclusion. However, Abernathy still needed to be done.

"Excellent! We're on the same wavelength, then!" Abernathy exclaimed, his voice ringing with excitement. "But what we can accomplish is far more significant, more earth-shattering. The only catch is that we must witness the crimes unfold in real-time. We tally the casualties and gauge if the crime is high-profile enough to warrant our intervention and rectification. This is the future Johnny Boy. We must correct free will mistakes and shape them to my desired mold."

"Correct it? As in, take the role of the divine?" John interjected, his voice rich with disbelief and dismay.

Abernathy nodded with an eerie calm voice, "In a manner of speaking, yes and no. We seize the reins of free will, sculpting it as per my design. Consider me as a co-creator, my young protege."

John sat there, his face etched with confusion, struggling to comprehend Abernathy's glorious vision.

"So, we're targeting celebrities? Professional athletes?" John queried, attempting to decipher Abernathy's cryptic words.

"Think bigger!" Abernathy retorted, his voice a cocktail of wit and audacity.

"I'm talking about mass atrocities that can devastate our youth, incite global panic, and undermine our beloved nation's foundations. Such acts of terror can fracture the unity of our country and shatter us. We must first allow events to take their course, respecting free will. But afterward, we wield power to reshape the narrative uniquely, modifying a fragment of the scenario so that, instead of losing thirty innocent lives, we only lose the bastard who sought to shatter existence for the innocents. Remember the mass shooting in Oklahoma that ignited riots and split our nation on gun control and racism? Of course, you don't because it never transpired. Instead, the would-be perpetrator hanged himself before executing his murderous plan - poetic justice. Simulation successful."

Abernathy paused, a smug grin playing on his lips, before continuing. "You're familiar with the concept of assisted suicide, correct?"

John nodded, his silent consent aiming to expedite the conversation.

"Dr. Kevorkian may no longer be with us, but his controversial legacy endures. It shouldn't be too challenging to convince a misguided teenager to end his life before he takes others'. The results we have observed with you have been phenomenal - you're on the brink of determining another's destiny on my command."

Abernathy's grin grew wider as John stood there, his face a mask of bewilderment, struggling to contain his escalating objections. John clenched his fists and ground his teeth, his frustration unmistakable.

John shouted dubiously, "This is practically murder! It would help if you madmen were held accountable and faced justice with a firing squad. I'd be honored to take the kill shot."

As Abernathy's voice resonated through the room, passionately embracing his radical notions and what seemed like sacrilege to John, a whirlwind of thoughts consumed his mind. The weight of the moral dilemma pressed upon him, and he couldn't help but long for Jane's presence at that moment.

In their shared moments, John and Jane had always been each other's sounding boards, their voices of reason and unwavering support. John wanted Jane's insight, her unique perspective that often shed light on angles he might have missed.

As Abernathy continued his emotional monologue, John's stoic silence masked a longing to share this moment with Jane, to seek her guidance and understanding. Her absence amplified the weight of the decisions he faced, leaving him to grapple with the moral implications alone.

The trauma of Jane's absence loomed over him, intertwining with the danger and uncertainty of his captivity. John's heart ached, knowing that his absence would surely take its toll on her, just as her absence weighed heavily on him. He longed to protect her from the pain, to shield her from the harsh reality of his imprisonment.

John knew that he had a duty not only to himself but also to Jane to uncover the truth and bring justice to those affected by the conspiracy. The thought of reuniting with her, of holding her in his arms once more, fueled his resolve to face the challenges ahead.

As Abernathy's voice faded into the background, John's focus sharpened. He knew that the decisions he made in this pivotal moment would shape not only his destiny but also the lives of countless others. And while the absence of Jane weighed heavily upon him, her unwavering love and support remained etched within his heart, providing the strength and courage needed to navigate the treacherous path ahead.

As he pondered the possibilities, beads of sweat formed on his forehead, reflecting his internal confusion. Could they harness this power to eradicate diseases like cancer to rewrite history? After intense reflection, John finally broke his silence; his voice imbued with curiosity and awe.

"How would you present such a\ argument to a panel of jury members? It would be quite the spectacle! The defense would need a spectacularly adept attorney to argue in favor of this approach. It sounds like something ripped straight from the pages of a science fiction novel, implausible and almost ludicrous. The jury would be compelled to question the sanity of the defense lawyer and the credibility of their argument. Wouldn't it be more beneficial to sacrifice one of my resources to discover a cure for cancer? Seems like a more productive use of our time since we've made little progress over the past three months with these absurd trials."

Abernathy's face lit up at John's words. "I'm thrilled you brought that up; therein lies the beauty!"

Abernathy punctuated his statement by slamming his fist on the table with passion.

"People neglect regular health check-ups, disregard symptoms, and abuse their bodies! We could eradicate cancer if everyone visited their doctor regularly. But here's what baffles me," Abernathy continued, his voice dropping to a contemplative tone, "when you first came onboard as a Subjector, you weren't capable of manipulation. It was only after the Subjective Protocol malfunctioned and required a reboot. That was the only unscheduled reboot in our history, and currently, we can do nothing to alter that."

Abernathy glanced up, a cunning glint in his eyes. "Nah, it's not worth the trouble," he dismissed, a nonchalant shrug of his shoulders. "A fifteen-minute data block was eradicated without a trace. Do you have any comments on that, Jimbo?" Abernathy posed the question, an air of knowing expectation in his tone. John met Abernathy's penetrating gaze and responded in a flat, emotionless voice.

"No, Sir, I am not privy to what you're referring to."

Abernathy seized his coffee mug and strolled towards the exit but abruptly stopped and swiveled around.

"You're nothing more than a deceitful, charming swindler," he spat, his voice seething with disdain.

"You can weave your web of lies all you wish, but the ongoing probe will eventually illuminate the truth. And guess what? Any external entity does not explicitly govern all our actions within these walls, save for the department under my supervision. As such, don't be taken aback if our investigative methods diverge from the conventional."

He paused, his lips twisting into a self-satisfied smirk. "The more adamant you prove to be, the more dismal your predicament becomes. But of course, you're already privy to that, aren't you, dullard?"

His laughter rang out, harsh and devoid of genuine delight. We would have identified you as a Subjector ages ago, and suddenly, your cerebral readings are skyrocketing! I'm convinced you orchestrated this anomaly. The guilt must be gnawing at your conscience. You relinquished your freedom for that foolish woman you wed, and now, you're being overpowered."

With a final, biting remark, Abernathy turned the key in the lock, the metallic click echoing ominously in the room, and exited, leaving John in solitude with his raging thoughts.

A wave of dread washed over him as he sat in the room, barely lit by the feeble glow of a lonely bulb. Abernathy's accusations held a kernel of truth - he had manipulated his brain readings to conceal his true identity as a Subjector.

Now, he was paying the price for his deception. But he refused to let Abernathy break him. He would find a way out of this and do whatever it takes to keep his family safe.

John finally calmed his brain down and dozed off in his chair. Late that night, John woke abruptly from a vivid nightmare, feeling anxious. For John to be accepted into the SPITE machine, perfect sleep was essential, so the thought of a sleepless night gave him significant anxiety.

Abernathy's words repeated in his mind, and he couldn't shake the idea of his actions. John knew the consequences of breaking the forbidden rule but had to see the truth

John accidentally adjusted the SPITE frequency to the night of his conception through his father's eyes, an event shrouded in mystery and unanswered questions.

As he did so, a wave of nausea washed over him, so potent that it seemed to resonate even in his father's consciousness. They did not conceive him that night and postponed the encounter the following evening.

He was the same man, with the same name and persona, but encased in a transformed facade. The mutation that had bestowed upon him the power to manipulate resulted from a temporal shift. This anomaly occurred post the timeline alteration.

He was seeking the truth about his father's mysterious past. Rumors and half-truths had always floated around, but John wanted to see firsthand what had transpired around that same period.

He yearned to understand his father better, to uncover the circumstances of his conception, and perhaps, in doing so, to learn more about his own identity.

However, rectifying this shift was beyond the realm of possibility. The sheer number of variables was overwhelming, and time was a luxury they were running short of. It was only a matter of time before someone would uncover the oddities at play.

John couldn't understand why, if he was so important as everyone claimed, he was allowed to kill himself. He had expected to be treated like a king, with much leverage and power at his disposal. So why should he care if he died when he didn't exist?

As he pondered these questions, John realized he had been manipulated. The people who claimed to be his allies used him for their purposes. They didn't care about him or his well-being - they only cared about what he could do for them.

With this realization, John knew he had to take matters into his own hands. He couldn't trust anyone but himself and needed to find a way to use his unique abilities to protect himself and those

he loved. He would no longer be a pawn in someone else's game -
he would be the one calling the shots.

The risks associated with employing the Subjective Protocol
Interface Terminal and Efficacy on distant kin, spanning as far
back as three generations, are widely considered unsafe.

However, the extent of the potential side effects remained
shrouded in mystery. A catastrophic incident during an
experimental trial caused an immediate halt in such procedures,
leading to their strict outlawing ever since. That had been over
twenty years ago, and John suspected that even Abernathy had
been oblivious to the specifics of the incident.

Nevertheless, John found himself confined, forbidden to return
home by the corrupt organization. The walls of his prison seemed
to mock him, a constant reminder of the power wielded by those
who sought to silence him.

Cut off from the world he once knew. John grappled with a
sense of isolation and despair. He hankered for the familiar
comforts of home, the warmth of his bed, and the simple pleasures

that had eluded him for far too long. The organization's grip tightened, holding him captive within the confines of their secret detention center.

Internally, he remains the same person, but externally, he is recognized as his "brother," and John, as an entity, ceases to exist. He is compelled by the state, government, and other regulatory bodies to renounce his identity as John.

John, as a legal individual, never was and never will be. Consequently, he is stripped of all rights. He can be detained indefinitely, and any action can be taken against him without facing any repercussions.

Should he lose his ability to manipulate, it would snuff out his will to live, and he wouldn't put it past someone as ruthless as Abernathy to eliminate him without a second thought.

As John struggled with the consequences of his actions and losing his identity, he knew he was running out of options. He had to find a way to stop Abernathy and the SPITE weapon. Still, he also had to protect Jane and ensure her safety. Torn between his love for Jane and his duty to save the world from Abernathy's sinister plans; John decided to take a desperate risk.

However, the plan backfired, leaving John trapped in a mutated body with no way to reverse the effects. Despite his altered appearance, John's love for Jane remained unchanged.

He knew he couldn't be with her in his current state, but he refused to give up on their relationship. He vowed to find a way to restore his humanity, even if it meant defying Abernathy and risking everything he held dear.

John's endeavors to thwart Abernathy escalated in their recklessness, fueled by desperation and the chilling realization of having nothing to lose. He was acutely aware that Abernathy wouldn't flinch at exploiting his mutated form against him, and the thought of endangering Jane was something he couldn't bear.

Amid the chaos, John stumbled upon a confidential document detailing the disastrous incident during the trial of the Subjective Protocol Interface Terminal and Efficacy on distant kin.

The revelation sent ripples of shock through the core of John's being as he grappled with the harsh truth. The technology he had endeavored to harness for the greater good was the instrument that obliterated countless lives. The weight of this realization bore down on him, a grim testament to the potential perils of unchecked power.

This newfound knowledge made John aware that he had to act swiftly and decisively. The sands of time were slipping through his fingers. With every passing second, Abernathy inched closer to unleashing the explosive force of the SPITE weapon.

He was compelled to unveil the truth and terminate Abernathy's reign of tyranny, but how could he accomplish such a feat when the law denied him a person?

Despite the seismic shifts in his past, Jane still recognized John as himself. It is believed that his new appearance would not affect Jane. While there remained much to uncover about this extraordinary phenomenon, she was under constant surveillance, scrutinized for any alterations in her thoughts, physical appearance, and behavior.

Despite the transformation of his identity, the moments they had shared remained untouched by time. He endeavored to convince the authorities of a fabricated identity, presenting himself as John's long-lost sibling, hoping that Jane would rekindle their love.

This request was denied immediately without an explanation. He yearned to perceive her once again through human eyes, to immerse himself in the myriad sensations her presence evoked. But all he could do was observe her through the eyes of his transformed self, a robotic canine.

John observed Jane from a distance, veiled behind the inconspicuous guise of a dog. Days had turned into an endless vigil, his eyes tracing her every move, committing her routines to his memory. He recognized the inherent risks of direct contact; it carried too great a danger for them both.

Yet, as he watched her, an ache of longing gnawed at his heart. He longed for her, for the melody of her voice and the affectionate gaze she once cast his way.

He knew of the bitter reality - he could no longer claim her as his own, not with the universal government surveillance shadowing his every move.

He was the product of a covert government experiment that had infused him with extraordinary abilities. However, these powers were a double-edged sword. In exchange, he was stripped of his humanity and, consequently, his rights.

He had attempted to reach out to Jane previously, but his actions had only invited trouble. The government had intercepted his efforts and had initiated surveillance on Jane. He couldn't afford to jeopardize her safety again.

Thus, he observed her from a distance, his heart brimming with a desperate yearning to be by her side again. Yet, he was painfully aware of the harsh reality - their reunion was impossible. He was a fugitive, a pariah deemed a menace to society. He was compelled to remain cloaked in the shadows, persistently staying on the move, slipping through the world's cracks unnoticed.

As he watched the retreating silhouette of Jane, a sense of resolve solidified within him. He knew, deep down, that he had made the correct choice. He couldn't gamble on her safety or let his urges endanger her.

He had to muster all his strength to continue in his struggle. It wasn't just for his sake but for Jane and countless others whom the government's secret experiments had wronged. His fight was their fight, his resistance a beacon of hope for justice and redemption.

# 14

Over several months, John had been tirelessly probing the scientific support of the phenomenon he found himself in, seeking to comprehend its functioning and the principles that drove it. Spotting an opportune moment when Abernathy's vigilance diminished, John seized the chance to gather crucial information.

As John stealthily moved through the facility, he whispered to himself under his breath a mantra of determination and focus. "Timing is everything," he murmured, reminding himself of the crucial moments he had to seize.

As he memorized the guards' patrol routes, he whispered their names softly, committing them to memory. "James... Sarah... Peter," he repeated, ensuring he wouldn't forget their identities and patterns.

While timing his movements, John whispered the countdown to himself, his voice barely audible. "Thirty-seven minutes... Just thirty-seven minutes," he muttered, reminding himself of his limited time to gather the needed information.

Approaching the mainframe room, his thoughts became more urgent, and his whispers intensified. "Almost there... Keep calm," he whispered, using his voice as a form of reassurance to steady his nerves.

Inside the mainframe, his whispered thoughts intensified. "Focus... Stay focused," he breathed, reminding himself to remain centered amidst the overwhelming information.

As he navigated through the digital pathways, John whispered his intentions, his voice barely audible in the room's silence. "Find the data... Capture the truth," he murmured, his words carrying purpose and determination.

With each passing moment, John's whispered thoughts became more urgent; his voice filled with excitement and caution. "Time is running out... Extract and retreat," he whispered, reminding himself of the impending deadline.

Emerging from the mainframe room, John's whispered words shifted to thoughts of escape. "Quiet footsteps... Leave no trace," he murmured, his voice barely audible as he planned his route back to safety.

Finally, in the solitude of his room, John whispered his reflections, his voice a soft murmur. "Another night of progress... But the madness continues," he whispered, acknowledging the small victories while understanding that the path to freedom was still long and uncertain.

He was deeply aware of the fatal consequences of a potential escape attempt. Hence the knowledge he gleaned remained securely nestled within the confines of his mind.

John's grasp of the technology was largely speculative, yet he fundamentally understood its workings. Each night, before going to bed, he would meticulously process the new data he had accumulated, attempting to piece together the mysterious puzzle that was the technology.

As John diligently chronicled his thoughts and discoveries in his secret journal, he also recorded crucial information about the technology of SPITE. The pages of the journal became a repository of his understanding, a tangible record of his quest for knowledge.

Within the journal's worn, weathered pages, John meticulously documented the workings of the technology. He described the intricate mechanisms and speculated on the underlying principles that allowed for the connection between consciousnesses. Diagrams and sketches adorned the pages, visual representations of his theories and deductions.

But the journal held more than just his interpretations of the technology. John also chronicled his observations of Abernathy, meticulously noting his patterns and behaviors. He watched Abernathy's every move, keenly aware of the man's routines and habits.

In the journal's pages, John detailed the precise moments when Abernathy entered passwords or input numbers into door locks. He carefully noted these sequences, piecing together the puzzle of Abernathy's digital security measures.

John's journal became evidence of his resourcefulness and determination with each observation and deduction. It was a record of his relentless pursuit of freedom as he sought to understand the technology that held him captive and the man who wielded it.

The journal became a treasure trove of information, safeguarded within the confines of his room. Its pages held the key to unlocking the secrets of both the technology and Abernathy's control, serving as a source of inspiration and a reminder of the information he needed to gather to secure his escape.

Journal Entry - Day 56:

"Today, I made a breakthrough in understanding the technology of SPITE. Through my analysis of various scientific literature, I believe the connected mammal must possess a cognitive capacity beyond basic survival instincts. The technology seems sensitive to a specific form of brainwave, indicating that higher-order thinking is necessary for the connection."

"My Thoughts: This discovery is significant. It confirms my suspicions that the technology requires a certain level of cognitive ability to function properly. It raises intriguing questions about the nature of consciousness and how it interacts with this remarkable system. I must delve deeper into the scientific literature to uncover more clues."

Journal Entry - Day 62:

"I have been closely observing Abernathy, studying his every move. Today, I witnessed him inputting a series of numbers into a door lock. I managed to memorize the sequence: 8-2-5-1. This could grant me access to restricted areas within the facility, allowing me to gather more information."

"My Thoughts: This is a breakthrough in itself. With this newfound knowledge, I have the means to explore areas that were previously inaccessible to me. It will require careful planning and precise timing, but the possibilities are promising. I must tread cautiously, ensuring Abernathy remains unaware of my activities."

Journal Entry - Day 68:

"I've been monitoring Abernathy's actions closely, and today, I noticed him typing his password on his computer. It was a combination of letters and numbers: "Spite@1923". This password could grant me access to confidential files and documents stored on his computer."

"My Thoughts: The password is a valuable piece of information. Accessing Abernathy's computer would provide me with a wealth of knowledge and potentially expose his true intentions. I must be patient and wait for the opportune moment to move. Timing will be crucial, as I cannot afford to be caught snooping around his personal files."

Journal Entry - Day 74:

"After careful observation, I have noticed a pattern in Abernathy's behavior. He seems to become more distracted during late-night hours, likely due to fatigue. This offers a window of opportunity for me to infiltrate the mainframe room undetected and gather essential data."

"My Thoughts: This is a significant breakthrough. The late-night hours provide the perfect cover for my covert operations. I must use this time wisely, ensuring I can gather as much information as possible without arousing suspicion. It will require careful planning and precise execution, but it is a risk worth taking in my quest for freedom."

Journal Entry - Day 139:

"Today, a remarkable revelation unfolded before my eyes, reshaping my understanding of the world I am confined within. Through a series of painstaking experiments and relentless exploration, I have uncovered the true nature of Dash, Abernathy's seemingly ordinary canine companion. Dash is not a mere machine, but a sophisticated creation intricately connected to the SPITE technology."

"In a stunning twist, I have discovered that I possess the ability to control Dash through the very same system that holds me captive. Through this peculiar connection, I can interact with Jane, the unknowable presence residing within the facility. Dash becomes the conduit, bridging the gap between us and offering me a glimpse of the outside world. It is unclear if anyone else can control him through the SPITE. I have seen Abernathy make commands to this puppy, but I never knew it was synthetic."

"The implications of this revelation are profound. It means that my only means of communication and connection lies in the realm of technology, bound within the confines of the SPITE machine. It raises questions about the true purpose behind this connection and the extent of Abernathy's knowledge and manipulation. Was this a clever ruse to get me to cooperate?"

"As I reflect upon this newfound understanding, a surge of determination courses through my veins. I must exploit this unique connection, utilizing Dash as a means to uncover the secrets that Abernathy guards so fiercely. Through this symbiotic relationship with Dash, I shall navigate the path towards freedom, unraveling the mysteries that bind us all within this horrific facility."

John meticulously documented his thoughts, observations, and strategies through his journal entries. The written words served as a roadmap to guide his actions and reflect his relentless pursuit of knowledge and freedom. Each entry held the potential to unlock new secrets and propel him closer to his ultimate goal.

Dash is primarily synthetic but natural enough to fool the average person. Constructed from canine D.N.A. with custom-made organs, a functioning brain, and a working nervous system, this dog believes it is a canine, sentient when disconnected through John. Mammals with inferior brain function are unable to imagine existential circumstances.

This one-hundred-million-dollar synthetic creature was created by the same people who eventually terminated the Subjectors from existence in any form. John discovered that Abernathy was the lead on the artificial dog, keeping Jane preoccupied from learning what happened to him.

The technology, he presumed, was sensitive to a specific form of brainwave, one potent enough to forge a connection, suggesting that the mammal must possess a cognitive capacity that transcended basic survival instincts such as feeding, sleeping, and procreation. While the SPITE is designed for simulation, John was convinced he was viewing either a current or past time.

There has been recorded data of connecting with a Chimpanzee, but it could have been a nearby Zookeeper. There has also been evidence of connections with a dolphin, but that could have been a very agile scuba diver.

As John reflected on Abernathy, he couldn't shake off a strong feeling of repulsion. Some may have seen him as a tyrant, while others may have viewed him as a saint, but to John, he was despicable. Whenever he saw Abernathy's face, he felt an overwhelming urge to grab it and squeeze it until it turned into a gooey mush he could shove down his throat.

Despite his hatred for Abernathy, John tried getting Jane to read his journal and understand his side of the story. But she always refused to stay for more than a few minutes, making it difficult for him to explain the truth. However, he knew that the contents of his journal could explain why he had gone missing.

On the night when Jane discovered the crawl space, Dash was on a mission to retrieve his second journal. He knew it held the key to his disappearance and could prove he hadn't willingly left. His curiosity had been too strong to pass up the opportunity to make a name for himself by discovering something new. But he had just realized the actual cost of his actions when it was too late. However, he retrieved the journal as Dash and placed it in his study while Jane was in the hospital.

Now, as he sat in his cell, John knew that he had to find a way to use his unique abilities to protect himself and his family. He refused to be a pawn in Abernathy's game and would do whatever it took to control his destiny.

# 15

"Rise and shine!" Abernathy exclaimed, his mischievous grin stretching across his face, his voice filled with a hint of excitement. "Today is a special day, my little minion. The sun's golden rays pierced through the curtains, casting a warm glow on Abernathy's face. The room was enclosed in a muted silence, interrupted only by the faint sounds of birds chirping outside.

Abernathy's eyes sparkled with a twisted delight as he continued, his words laced with chilling anticipation.

"There was a tragic incident over the weekend, a mass shooting that shattered thirty-five lives. The air reeked of gunpowder, mingling with the scent of fear and desperation. Blood stained the floors, its metallic aroma lingering in the air. At the same time, bodies lay strewn about, a haunting montage of devastation. Can you believe it?"

John's voice, heavy with resignation, cut through the tense atmosphere.

"I know where this is going," he muttered, his words barely audible amidst the weight of despair. The room seemed to grow colder as if echoing John's inner turmoil.

"What if I refuse?"

"Funny you should ask," a twisted smile on his lips. His voice carried a mocking edge as if relishing the power he held.

"I will answer your questions with a question. What happens when you dare to disobey? Or better yet, what happens if you dare to exploit your privileged position? How many would kill for the opportunity you have?" Abernathy's words hung in the air, thick with taunting implications.

John's voice trembled with despair, his words filled with desperate defiance. "I cannot bear the weight of such responsibility on my conscience. I acknowledge the tragedy and the pain it has caused, but I had no part in it, you despicable fool!"

Abernathy's tone shifted, laced now with a menacing undertone. "That's where you're mistaken. Are you trying to claim that you will willingly abandon the chance to save thirty-five lives?"

His voice dripped with a threatening tone, his anger simmering beneath the surface. "Nice insult! That takes courage, my friend. The courage that could easily be crushed, your life extinguished, as swiftly as carving a jack-o-lantern from your torso!"

John stood his ground, and his voice laced with defiance. "Your empty threats and arrogant demeanor only reveal the sad vulnerability of a pathetic child, bartering away all that is valuable for a Twinkie."

Abernathy interrupted, his voice rising to a manic pitch. "Okay, Sherlock, have you forgotten? Have you? ' He burst into maniacal laughter, his grip on sanity slipping.

"I have you cornered, my dear boy. Better pick up that bouquet of oopsie-daisies! Remember dear Jane? I graciously allowed you to be with her from the kindest of my heart. But not only can I take that away, but I can also unleash the Dog as a weapon, who would gladly extinguish her life with a mere press of a button! You constantly forget who holds the reins here, and I feel like a broken record trying to explain it to a damn toddler. How difficult can it be?

"It's pretty simple. You follow my orders and can continue your time with the miserable woman and her mutt." Abernathy chuckled, wiping away the tears of laughter with his stained shirt. "But let me entertain you with something even more delightful, my dear Sherlock," Abernathy continued, his grin widening with sadistic pleasure.

"You see that charismatic 'vet,' Dr. Argow, who has been charming your precious Jane? Well, here's the kicker: he's no vet at all. In fact, I hired him, an actor playing the part, to toy with your emotions. Oh, I've derived joy from watching your face twist with jealousy whenever he's near her! It's been a delicious spectacle for me, witnessing your torment."

Abernathy leaned in closer, his eyes gleaming with a twisted satisfaction. The room seemed to close in on John, suffocating him with the weight of his feebleness. The faint scent of Abernathy's cologne mixed with the sour taste of animosity in the air, intensifying the atmosphere of manipulation.

"So, Sherlock," Abernathy whispered, his voice dripping with spite. "I control every part of your existence, even those you believed were beyond my reach. Never forget who holds the strings here. Now, be a good little puppet and obey my commands, or risk losing everything you hold dear."

John sat silently, his heart heavy, knowing of his impending defeat. He felt broken, stripped of support, and utterly helpless. Abernathy's dominance loomed over him like a suffocating shadow, casting doubt on any hope of resistance.

His love for Jane burned within him, a flame fueled by desire and fear of losing her again. Yet, a part of him couldn't help but believe that he would never lay eyes on her again.

"Wake up, Johnny boy! Today is the day!" Abernathy's voice boomed through the room. His words were laced with twisted anticipation, his tone filled with sadistic pleasure. The air crackled with a charged energy as if the room held its breath, waiting for the impending manipulation to unfold.

"We finally get to witness just how efficient you can be in manipulation," Abernathy continued, his voice dripping with disapproval.

His words hung in the air, heavy with a threatening sense of judgment. Abernathy's vile smirk twisted his features, casting a shadow over his face.

"I assume you will fail miserably," he taunted, relishing the prospect of terminating their relationship. "Hence the word 'terminate.' The word rolled off Abernathy's tongue with a hostility that sent shivers down John's spine. The room seemed to darken, the shadows dancing with malicious intent.

"But," Abernathy's tone suddenly shifted a trace of anticipation, tainting his words, "if things go well, we can move on to the next

phase. We can shape history itself. Are you ready, Johnny boy?"
The weight of Abernathy's words settled on John's shoulders, a
heavy burden that threatened to crush his resolve.

John had been awake for hours, his mind consumed by restless
thoughts that refused to grant him a pardon. The torment of
contemplating the ethics of assisted suicide had plagued him
throughout the night, leaving him weary and disoriented.

He had spent countless hours trying to justify the toll it would
take on his fragile mental state, desperately seeking a way to prove
his worth. If he could demonstrate that he was the only Subjector
capable of success through multiple trials, perhaps he could secure
more privileges, a glimmer of control in the suffocating darkness
of this twisted experiment.

"I am ready," John replied, his voice steady despite his
uproar—determination burned in his eyes, a flickering flame that
refused to be extinguished.

"What, no smart-ass remark or moral compass mumbo jumbo?" Abernathy's voice dripped with sarcasm, his words laced with a bitter edge.

John's response was swift, devoid of hesitation. He stood up abruptly, his movements purposeful and resolute. Putting on the red jumpsuit, he zipped it up swiftly, deliberately avoiding the sensitive area of his Adam's apple. Abernathy gave him a light shove, a reminder of their power dynamic, as he guided John toward the room that housed the SPITE.

The air within the room felt colder than usual, a chilling sensation that seeped into John's bones. Goosebumps prickled his skin, and a tremor ran through his body, betraying the fear that clung to him like a second skin.

Entering the machine, John was submerged in darkness, the absence of light amplifying his unease. He laid his head down on the cushioned surface, his body tense with anticipation.

As the headpiece settled, he felt a light pressure against his temples. John obediently put on the oxygen mask, its cool touch against his skin a blatant contrast to the suffocating atmosphere of the room. The SPITE, an imposing presence in the darkness, must be sealed, silent, and pitch dark to achieve its maximum effectiveness.

Agent Piccolo entered the room, adding an extra layer of tension. Holding a tablet, he stood beside Abernathy, his finger gliding up and down the screen as he searched for specific data. The soft hum of electronic devices filled the room, mingling with the hushed anticipation in the air.

"Do you possess the brainwave readings from that despicable waste of life, the one who mercilessly butchered all those innocent people?" Abernathy's voice dripped with a mix of disgust and curiosity. The words hung in the air like a foul stench, tainting the atmosphere with their malice.

"Yes, sir, we executed the express protocol," Agent Piccolo responded, his voice tinged with concern.

"Express? Goodness, one would think this wretched kid was the freaking president!" Abernathy's voice dripped with doubt. He shook his head in a mixture of disgust and condescension.

"It's sickening," he muttered, his words laced with bitter contempt. "J.F.K.'s readings took three times as long to obtain, and all he seemed to do was die," Abernathy continued.

He scoffed, a pompous chuckle escaping his lips. "Obtaining these readings as our top priority seems like a rather easy decision, don't you think?" Agent Piccolo, seemingly unaffected, continued to busy himself, feigning deafness to Abernathy's words.

"Very well, these are the coordinates to the shooter's precise consciousness, and these are for the subconscious," Agent Piccolo announced, his voice a mere whisper in the tense silence that shrouded the room. His words hung in the air, pregnant with the weight of the impending experiment.

"No," Abernathy interjected, his voice filled with a predatory gleam, "I want to witness the true extent of our power. Johnny Boy has exhibited potential that surpasses anything we have ever encountered."

The words dripped with a stubborn excitement, a hunger to test the limits of their creation. Abernathy's voice held an unsettling mixture of anticipation and hostility as if reveling in the prospect of unleashing chaos and manipulation upon their unsuspecting subject.

"But, Sir," Agent Piccolo interjected cautiously, his voice tinged with worry, "bypassing the subconscious's exploration, we risk conducting a flawed simulation.

A mere imperfection could render the entire trial futile, preventing us from comprehending the intricate circumstances that drive someone to commit such heinous acts." His words hung in the air, a delicate plea for reason amidst the storm of Abernathy's determination.

"I am well aware of the potential consequences," Abernathy responded sternly, his voice commanding authority.

"It is a risk I am willing to take." The words were mixed with a chilling resolve as if Abernathy saw himself as untouchable, impervious to failure. "I will pretend your lack of judgment was merely a momentary brain lapse!" Abernathy's voice rose, the words tinged with biting mockery.

"Do you think I am oblivious to these risks? I want to witness him fail, to have the justification to put this mongrel to sleep. Do you understand?"

The words dripped with contempt, a toxic disregard for their subject. "Decades of tireless effort, all in pursuit of what John seemingly possesses." The bitterness in Abernathy's voice was evident.

"And so," Abernathy continued, his voice a sharp blade cutting through the tension, "am I supposed to believe that we have stumbled upon this miraculous child I am now meant to worship? Skip the subconscious exploration, label it a failed attempt, and plunge headfirst into his conscious mind."

The words were delivered with piercing cynicism, a cruel mockery of the supposed significance of their endeavor.

"Ye-, Yes, sir," Agent Piccolo responded softly. The weight of Abernathy's authority pressed down upon him, suffocating any facade of opposition.

John's senses were assaulted as he entered the virtual realm. The air crackled with static, surrounding him in a disorienting haze. Electronic pulses coursed through his body, causing his muscles to vibrate with nervous energy. It was as if an invisible force was manipulating his mind, leaving him electrified and unnerved.

As the static began to dissipate, John's surroundings materialized before him. The scene that unfolded before his eyes was bleak and disheartening. Dirty sheets clung to a worn-out bed while a sea of empty Dr. Pepper cans littered the floor. The realization struck him like a punch to the gut - he had found himself in the shooter's bedroom.

A surge of emotions washed over John, drowning him in a whirlpool of anger, frustration, and mental defeat. It felt like happiness existed in an elusive realm beyond his grasp, an inaccessible subclass of survival. His mind struggled to comprehend the weight of these emotions, overwhelmed by their intensity.

His attention was drawn to a hand raised and clutching a phone. Time appeared to slow as he focused, willing himself to see the date and time. And then, in a fleeting moment, he witnessed the truth. The date marked two weeks before the horrifying carnage that would ensue. It couldn't be a coincidence, John pondered, his thoughts swirling with confusion and disbelief.

The shooter's movements were precise and deliberate as he aimed his gun. However, a bullet accidentally escaped the gun and landed on the bed. The shooter quickly corrected his mistake by retrieving the round and returning it to its chamber. The weapon was now fully loaded and ready to unleash its deadly potential.

John was caught in a vortex of emotions he had never experienced. The shooter's pain resonated through every fiber of his being. It was a pain so consuming and unbearable that thoughts of suicide invaded John's mind. The only perceived escape from such torment was unconsciousness or death.

Desperate, he pleaded, trembling, "Put the gun down, unload it. Put the gun down, unload it."

With a chilling dread, John watched the shooter turn off the safety, pointing the gun towards his forehead. Panic surged through him, a primal fear gripping his heart.

"Oh God, please, no. Please! I don't want to die, please, God," John pleaded silently, his voice drowned by the cacophony of his racing thoughts. His gaze fixated upon the gun barrel as if staring into his demise.

Then, a flicker of movement caught John's attention. A silhouette emerged in the doorway, approaching the scene. Time seemed to hang suspended, each passing second stretching into perpetuity.

The shooter aimed the gun at the shadowy figure, poised to unleash a devastating act of violence. John's heart pounded in his chest, and his breath caught in his throat.

In a desperate attempt to intervene, John's voice erupted in desperation.

"Stop!" he shouted, his plea slicing through the tension-laden air.

The figure froze momentarily, then lunged towards the gun, desperate to prevent the impending tragedy. In the next moment, everything embarked into darkness, leaving John in a state of confusion.

As the simulation ended, the SPITE system began to retract its hold on John's senses. The indifferent air brushed against his skin, the sudden chill contrasting with the dampness of his sweat-soaked body. He was hyperventilating, his heart pounding like a trapped animal desperate for escape.

Abernathy's voice, dripping with sarcasm, cut through the heavy atmosphere, momentarily breaking the spell of terror that had gripped John. He began to relax slowly, his breathing gradually steadying and his vitals returning to normalcy.

"That was the most nightmarish experience of my life!" John exclaimed, his voice trembling. Tears welled up in his eyes as he spoke. His words struggled to get out.

"No one should ever have to endure such terror. It was nothing but irrational fear, awakened by the demons of the past."

His words hung heavy in the air, a testament to the permanent impact of the shooter's memories and visions. John's voice cracked with raw emotion as he continued, "I, I- I'm haunted. I was consumed by darkness. I was the devil in that chair, witnessing the most dreadful aspects of my childhood. This kid, he was abused and cast aside by his own family. Society rejected him, leaving him to find solace in online hate and far-right ideologies. So much needless animosity. Those memories, those visions, will forever haunt me, even though they were not my own."

His voice dripped with sarcasm as he turned to Agent Piccolo. "That is dark even for you, Johnny boy," he scoffed, his gaze fixated on Piccolo, who remained engrossed in his tablet, waiting for crucial data on the incident. "He's still in jail. No change."

The shock on Abernathy's face transformed into a cruel grin, a sinister pleasure derived from being proven right. "What! I was right!" he exclaimed mockingly, his voice tinged with triumph. "John here is just a mediocre Subjector like all the others. Hallelujah! We can finally move on from this nonsense and continue the path that was created by yours truly. We can finally focus on controlling history as it was meant to. By me!"

Observing the exchange, Piccolo crumpled his brow in confusion. Abernathy's gaze shifted, recognizing the perplexed expression on Piccolo's face. Sensing an opportunity to assert his dominance, Abernathy demanded an explanation. "Something you want to tell me?"

Piccolo hesitated, his voice filled with uncertainty as he relayed his findings. "I cannot find any information or reference to the shooting in the media," he admitted. "I am also cross-checking some of the victims' Facebook pages, and there are posts, including pictures and time stamps after they were allegedly murdered. How is this possible?"

Abernathy's anger flared, a fiery blaze consuming his features. His face flushed, a crimson hue spreading across his cheeks.

"Then why the hell is that prick in jail?" he seethed, his voice laced with venom. The intensity of his frustration radiated from him, filling the room with tension.

"Well, according to the police records," Piccolo began, his voice measured as he relayed the information. "He fired a shot in his room, and the neighbor called the police. Unlawful discharge of a firearm. Attempted manslaughter."

Piccolo's words carried a weight, each syllable punctuating the severity of the shooter's actions. "When questioned by the police, he said that his mind kept telling him to kill himself, but other parts of his mind wanted to put the gun down. When confronted, he thought about pulling the trigger and did it by accident. After failing some tests, he is now under psychiatric evaluation and is considered a danger to society. Possibly an indefinite stay in a mental hospital."

Abernathy's fury burned brighter. His gaze fixated on John with an intensity that could sear through steel. "Want to tell me something, Johnny?" he spat, his voice dripping with bitterness.

"Please help me understand what happened there. Because last I checked, your orders were either to fail or get that monster to kill himself!"

John's throat tightened, his heartbeat thundering in his ears as he struggled to find his voice. The weight of Abernathy's words bore down on him, threatening to crush his spirit.

"You have no idea what I went through in there," he managed to say, his voice trembling with fear and anger. "You heartless sociopath! It felt so real, and I did not want to die. I am sorry."

Abernathy's eyes narrowed his expression into a mask of contempt. "You are sorry, huh?" The hatred in his words hung heavy in the air, poisoning the atmosphere with his anger.

Interrupting the tense exchange, Piccolo interjected, holding a tablet for Abernathy to see. "You really need to see this, sir," he urged, his voice tinged with urgency. Abernathy tore his gaze away from John and glanced at the tablet, his face contorting with intrigue and frustration.

"What did you want to show me?" Abernathy demanded, his voice laced with impatience as he turned to Agent Piccolo.

Piccolo hesitated, his eyes gleaming with excitement as he presented the information. "Well, Sir, John was on the same frequency as the shooter within a few seconds of entering his consciousness," he explained. "What is even more incredible is the similar consistency throughout the time he was there. Look, not once did the conscious frequency break off into tangents."

Abernathy's brows furrowed in confusion. "What the hell are you saying?" he asked, his voice tinged with frustration.

"This was not a simulation, Abernathy," Piccolo clarified, his tone filled with awe. "Our best Subjectors will average one-thousand tangents per minute, making the manipulation more of a

305

lottery as we know. We have something special here, and I have already sent the data to our main headquarters. He is the one, Sir. This, this is absolutely remarkable."

Abernathy stared blankly, his mind struggling to process the implications of Piccolo's words. "Son of a bitch," he muttered, anger and resignation seeping into his voice. He knew that his power was quickly depleting, and all his hard work was about to be ruined by John, someone he held no respect for. Turning back to John, Abernathy dismissed him with a cold command. "Get out of my sight; I will deal with you later. Back to your cage, pig."

John's heart sank, the weight of Abernathy's words pressing down on him like an invisible force. He left the room abruptly, his emotions whirling with confusion and despair. Two agents escorted him back to his room, their presence a constant reminder of his captivity.

As he lay in bed, curled up in a ball, his mind spiraled with thoughts of what had transpired in the SPITE. The events felt hauntingly real, leaving him traumatized and unable to shake the vivid memories from his mind.

It was difficult for John to comprehend people's struggles with overwhelming emotions. He had only been a part of it for a few minutes, yet the impact lingered, searing into his consciousness. John replayed those last few seconds in the SPITE on a loop in his head, the images imprinted into his memory. Despite the mayhem, he found comfort in knowing that because of his actions, there were no casualties due to a reckless decision. He had altered that reality, allowing the victims to continue living and to seize the opportunities life presented them.

"Everything all right, sir?" Piccolo asked Abernathy with a concerned look on his face.

"What do you think, genius?" Abernathy snarled, his frustration boiling over. "I was the Elite Subjector with the fewest tangents and first pick for higher profile cases, and now this pretty boy shows up, and I am stuck babysitting the little teat sucker."

"I can understand the frustration, sir," Piccolo replied cautiously, "but your abilities have been waning for some time now and almost vanished around the time he showed up."

"And you think that was some coincidence?" Abernathy responded, his voice filled with bitterness.

"Are you sure this isn't a part of the simulation? Riverdale mentioned the ability to change the past, but I should have taken him seriously. I mean, come on, do you know how insane that sounds? Are you trying to tell me we have successfully accessed the fourth dimension and revisited actual moments in time?"

"We have to assume, yes. There is no evidence to prove otherwise," Piccolo reasoned, his voice tinged with uncertainty.

Abernathy's frustration escalated, his anger manifesting in a violent act. He grabbed a nearby chair and hurled it against the fiberglass wall, the impact shattering the chair into pieces while the fiberglass remained intact. Piccolo stood frozen in shock and fear, unsure of what would happen next.

"No evidence? I do not need evidence!" Abernathy exclaimed, his voice filled with desperation.

"I was a God to you people! That ass-wipe in the other room conjugated that power unlawfully, and now he does not even want it. That power will be wasted; John has no idea what to do with it or the potential."

Before Abernathy could continue his rant, Agent Riverdale entered the room, his expression puzzled. "What the hell happened here?" he asked, his voice tinged with annoyance.

Abernathy started to speak, but Riverdale cut him off dismissively.

"You know what, I do not care," his voice dripping with condescension.

"Have you seen Subjector Y's latest results? Astounding. We never thought this to be possible. Hey, Abernathy, remember when we thought you would be the one to do this? Y has shown remarkable improvement, while yours continues to decline. We made the right decision to replace you. You are a much better fit with your current duties anyway."

Abernathy avoided Riverdale's gaze, his anger simmering beneath the surface. He knew that if Riverdale knew how he felt about John, he could be removed from the case and downgraded to a mundane desk job. He assembled the last strength to keep himself from another outburst, silently seething with unspoken resentment.

"I see you are just as flabbergasted as me," Riverdale continued, oblivious to Abernathy's internal havoc. "I want you to make sure he is well taken care of. We cannot risk him trying to escape by suicide and ensure he gets more time with Dash. Keep him happy, whatever it takes."

Abernathy nodded, his face a mask of forced compliance. Deep down, however, he vowed to find a way to regain his power and prove that he was the superior Subjector. The battle for control was far from over.

"Yes sir," Abernathy replied through gritted teeth, his frustration evident.

The next day, John woke up to the sound of his alarm, feeling a sense of unease. Something was different about the routine. Abernathy barged into the room before he could fully process it, his demeanor even more off than usual. John felt a surge of fear, his body tensing up as he awaited Abernathy's words.

"We are doing things a little differently today," Abernathy said, surprisingly calm. "You have been authorized to spend the day as Dash. The SPITE is ready for you."

John's confusion grew. Spending time with Jane as Dash was something he always cherished, but there was an underlying feeling of hesitation. Despite this, his desire to be with Jane overpowered any doubts. He couldn't understand why his feelings were conflicted.

As Abernathy spoke, John noticed a strange civility in his tone, as if someone else was pulling the strings. A sense of paranoia crept over him, making his thoughts distorted and confusing. He had an intense urge to resist the orders, suspecting Abernathy of playing some sick joke on him.

Unable to contain his irritation, John closed his eyes tightly and aggressively ran his hand through his hair. The repetitive motion escalated into a mini tantrum of exasperation. He sat there for several minutes, trying to make sense of his swirling thoughts and contemplating every possible scenario.

The paranoia intensified, making it difficult for John to distinguish between his thoughts and Abernathy's manipulations. He questioned whether these doubts were genuine or a result of Abernathy's schemes. The uncertainty weighed heavily on his mind as he grappled with whether to follow orders or trust his instincts.

# 16

Abernathy retreated from the room abruptly, his departure as sudden as a summer storm, leaving the door slightly unhinged and the jumpsuit poised in silent invitation. John reacted with urgency, putting on the intriguing garment with a quickness born of raw anticipation.

He was resolved not to squander such a precious opportunity - a day in Jane's company was like a day in paradise, a sweet escape from the dreary, and he was committed to savoring every fleeting moment.

John's mind was a whirlwind of contemplation, meticulously evaluating the wisest allocation of this precious time. He knew he needed to act shrewdly while guardedly evading unwanted scrutiny. He wanted Jane to grasp the depth of their situation, either reconcile with it or find a semblance of closure.

He tried to picture the agony she must be experiencing, and the idea of her in such distress filled him with a deep sense of shared pain. He compared her suffering to a mother whose child had mysteriously disappeared, drowning her in a sea of sorrow and uncertainty.

John sprang into the confines of the SPITE. As the hatch began its descent, closing him in, he felt the specter of past trauma creeping in, inducing a surge of panic. This panic gave birth to a claustrophobic sensation, a feeling of being trapped that he had never encountered before.

He shut his eyes tightly, focusing intensely on the rhythmic pulse of his breath, a lifeline to prevent any alarms from sounding off and prematurely ending his mission.

Gradually, he reclaimed his mental fortitude, and his sense of normality began to seep back in. His eyes sprung open, a renewed glint of determination in their depth. "Show time," John murmured, a whisper filled with anticipation and resolve.

John registered a sudden clarity as the static lifted. His senses are now alert to the minute nuances of his environment. He observed the intricate mosaic of the kitchen floor tiles, their patterns as unique as individual fingerprints. Meanwhile, Jane was utterly absorbed in the digital world her phone projected, a spoon held aimlessly in her hand.

Time, precious and fleeting, was a critical factor; he needed to divert her attention and guide her towards his office, the secret resting place of his journal placed securely on top of his safe.

Compared to the complexity of human behavior, controlling Dash was as effortless as turning a key in a lock, an action John could initiate without hesitation.

The speed with which thought transitioned into action was breathtaking. Assuming control over Dash, he maintained a cautious distance and masterfully orchestrated the dog to squat, indicating imminent urination on the floor. Jane's response was instinctive, a gut reaction born of domestic habit, and she rose from her seat with an enthusiasm that mirrored her sudden urgency.

With a hint of amusement, she commanded, "Outside!" As she made a beeline towards Dash, John adeptly directed the canine through the hallway, around a concealed bend, and into the sanctuary of his office.

Dash, now standing on his hind legs, scrabbled at the doorknob with an intensity that soon led to its capitulation under relentless pressure.

Jane paused at the threshold, her hand hesitating on the now open door to John's room. It had been a considerable time since she had ventured into this private space, and the flood of memories associated with her beloved stirred a complex cocktail of emotions within her.

As she cautiously stepped into the room, she took in the sight of his belongings. Each object is a silent testament to his existence, preserved in its original place as if frozen in time.

Her eyes roamed the room, her mind painting illusions of her husband's presence as she was swimming in a sea of nostalgia. She allowed herself to be swept away in the tide of reminiscence, revisiting the shared moments of joy that had exhaled life into her room.

Dash frolicked about the room, his snout eagerly exploring the unfamiliar territory. Suddenly, as if latching onto a specific aroma, his demeanor shifted to one of single-minded resolve, and he began to follow the scent trail with unwavering focus. It was only a short time before his search culminated in discovering an inconspicuous journal resting on top of the safe.

The dog pawed at the journal, inviting his human companion to explore the hidden narratives within its pages. His canine grin showed an almost impish understanding as if recognizing the significance of the treasure he had unearthed. Jane, a mix of curiosity and apprehension playing across her face, held the journal tentatively.

Dash seemed to pick up on her reluctance and nudged at her arm with an insistent nudge, his body language urging her to delve into the written records.

Finally succumbing to the silent encouragement, she cracked open the journal and embarked on the journey within its pages. The emotions of her missing husband seemed to originate from the inked words.

She was moved, finding relief in the intimate thoughts of her love, and gratitude welled within her for her canine companion. Dash's gentle insistence had led her to this personal connection, a bridge across the chasm of loss built from the pages of a forgotten journal.

Jane was overwhelmed when she started to read the personal journal. She had no idea what to expect, and the sheer amount of information was almost too much to bear. She knew she had to keep calm and read it carefully, but her heart pounded as she navigated through the data.

The information was organized in different sections starting with Abernathy's dossier.

"This bastard Abernathy is holding you hostage? Why can't you esca... Oh, the collar." Jane continued reading through the details. "John, what did you get yourself into?"

She was determined to uncover the truth, but the daunting task made even the bravest soul's quiver. Jane was shocked to discover the unethical practices her husband had been secretly engaging in after reading the damning information.

She had always known he had been working in secrecy for the government but never realized it had been to such a questionable degree. It was a difficult realization for her to come to terms with, but she knew she had to be honest with herself and face the truth of the situation.

"Hold up, assisted suicide? 'Mission failed, subject still alive.' This... this is horrible."

Jane was stunned after unearthing a secret of condemning proportions. Uncertainty swirled around her like a fog, the newfound knowledge resting on her shoulders like an unwieldy load. Amid the turmoil, she paused, gathering the scattered fragments of her thoughts to forge a path through the commotion.

With an aspect of calm, Jane plunged into extensive research, meticulously centering on the relevant laws and regulations. She aimed to decipher the most practical course of action, a roadmap to navigate her through this unexpected terrain.

Subsequently, she started weaving a strategic web, envisioning ways to wield information as a powerful tool. She had no intention of letting this unstable secret detonate prematurely; instead, she aimed to commandeer its potential to her advantage.

Energized with renewed purpose, Jane propelled herself forward, the wheels of her plan beginning to turn. She was determined to seize control of the situation and transform this unexpected revelation into a stepping stone rather than a stumbling block.

Sitting alone in the dim light of her home office, Jane felt a cold shiver run down her spine. "How could he?" she whispered, her voice barely audible. Her hands felt icy as she ran them over the damning documents again. "I knew he was working for the government secretly, but this...this is something else."

A wave of hopelessness washed over her, her stomach knotting. This was not the man she thought she knew. She could taste the bitter tang of betrayal. "I have to face this," she murmured, gripping the edge of the desk as if anchoring herself in the storm of her emotions.

In the room's silence, she could hear the soft rustle of papers as she organized her thoughts. The burden of this revelation weighing heavily on her, she braced herself for the journey ahead. "I need a plan," she voiced aloud, her words slicing through the stillness.

Determinedly, she dove into stacks of laws and regulations, her eyes scanning each line with meticulous care. She could almost smell the musty scent of old legal texts as she sought a practical way forward.

She began mapping out a strategy, visualizing how to use this damning information to her advantage. "I won't let this secret explode just yet," she told herself, her voice firm and resolute. As she prepared for the upcoming challenge, she noticed the tension in her muscles.

Jane's thoughts were consumed by her perception of John as a man. He was multilayered, his talents as diverse as a rainbow and a wit as keen as the edge of a finely honed blade. He was a loyal companion to those closest to him till the end.

His spirit would continue to resonate in the hearts of those who held his memory dearly. He had imprinted a permanent inscription on the lives he had touched, and his memory would linger like a beloved melody in the hearts of those he had deeply impacted.

Jane found anchorage in the memories she had created with John. She realized that his teachings and distinctive kindness had impacted her, his influence persisting beyond his physical absence. Jane knew she would always desire John's presence, but she was deeply grateful for their shared journey and the memories that time could never erase.

As she delved deeper into the journal, she discovered it was Pandora's box, concealing secrets that John had safeguarded for years. With each page she turned, her world seemed to fracture slightly.

The journal was a cryptic chronicle of his past, revelations about their marriage, and even musings about the children he had dreamt of. The realization that her husband had disguised so much from her was a bitter pill.

Yet, as she continued to navigate the muddle of inked secrets, Jane understood the need for caution in handling this explosive information. She was determined not to leap to hasty conclusions or make impulsive decisions that could seed regret. Instead, she allowed herself to digest the newfound knowledge and strategize her subsequent steps.

Jane sank next to Dash, initiating a one-sided conversation about the SPITE project, the lethal collar, and the government's unnerving ability to manipulate historical events. "Do you comprehend their abilities?" she posed the rhetorical question to her canine companion.

"They can rewrite the past, obliterate memories, and puppeteer people's minds. It's all part of their grand scheme to retain dominance and control." Jane was left reeling from the surprise.

"Well... theoretically speaking. This can't poss... How is all of this possible? Is John truly alive?"

At Jane's rhetorical inquiry, Dash let out an empathetic yelp, almost as if comprehending the gravity of her words.

"The collar was merely a cog in the intricate machinery of their structure," Jane explained, a grim undertone seeping into her voice.

"They were prepared to throw countless lives into the sacrificial fire to realize their ambitions. We cannot stand idle and let them succeed. We must prevent their plans." She let her words hang in the air for a beat, her mind drifting in the ocean of contemplation. "I just pray we're not too late," she added, a hint of anxiety in her voice.

Dash's ensuing yelp seemed to reverberate with reassurance, a canine affirmation that they still had a shot at victory.

In her continued exploration, Jane unearthed a game-changing revelation. She stumbled upon a document, a relic from the collar's architect left behind. John must have extracted this information from the confines of his incarcerated facility.

The paper was a trove of knowledge detailing the collar's wireless connectivity and the method to deactivate it. It also sheds light on the robotic dog's role, designed to interact with the collar through wireless means, rendering it the sole entity capable of immobilizing the device. The journal further expounded on a failsafe mechanism, stating that the dog had to function autonomously for the collar to be armed.

Jane's eyes fixated on Dash, her face a canvas of perplexity. The realization hit her like a lightning bolt: Dash, the figure before her, was not real. A surge of unease coursed through her veins as she desperately sought answers.

"John, are you somehow inhabiting this form?" she questioned, her voice filled with uncertainty.

Dash met her gaze, his affirmation communicated through a subtle nod. The weight of the truth pressed upon Jane, leaving her gasping for air as she sought to process the bewildering circumstances unfolding around her. A break was necessary, allowing her to collect herself and absorb the overwhelming sensations that enveloped her being.

"We must devise a strategy to halt their maneuverings, and we must do so before it's too late," Jane asserted, her voice reverberating with an unshakeable determination.

# 17

A sudden realization struck Jane like a wave crashing on the shore - Dash was the crucial piece in the puzzle of John's survival. As she dug deeper into the mystery, she came across a set of coordinates, presumably pinpointing John's hidden place of captivity.

With a sense of urgency, she quickly keyed the longitude and latitude figures into her Google search bar, her heart pounding in anticipation of revealing a secret location in some distant corner of the globe.

To her utter astonishment, the digital map that materialized pointed to no secret facility but her residence. Jane stared at the screen, her mind a whirlwind of confusion as she tried to piece together the puzzle. Memories flooded back of trailing Dash around the corner of the house and descending into a concealed crawl space.

"Could it have been real? The Bunker? Could the solution be that straightforward?" Jane questioned herself, her thoughts a flowing waterfall of realization and disbelief.

Jane's heart vibrated with a panicky tempo as she comprehended the possibility that the key to her husband's disappearance, the rescue mission for John, might have been nestled beneath her home all along. Knowing that time was of the essence.

She rapidly devised a plan to stealthily infiltrate the concealed crawl space and locate the mysterious bunker. She bided her time until the blanket of nightfall provided the perfect concealment for her undercover operation.

As she went through the dirt tunnel with Dash following closely behind, she felt her heart racing urgently. This time, she had an additional flashlight and a priceless journal.

Upon reaching the bunker that Dash led her to, she was confronted with a keypad, an obstacle she had no recollection of.

"Did I overlook a keypad?" she questioned herself, a thread of uncertainty weaving through her thoughts. She desperately skimmed through the pages of the journal, her fingers trembling with anxiety, hunting for a numerical sequence. She punched in the first code she stumbled upon, and to her astonishment, the keypad responded with an affirmative beep, granting her access to the bunker's interior.

As she cautiously stepped into the dimly lit space, her eyes gradually adjusted to the soft glow. What greeted her was an intricate control panel adorned with an array of buttons and levers. Dominating the scene was a large screen displaying a geographical map of the surrounding area.

Abruptly, the screen flickered, ushering in a message that sent a chill down her spine: "Welcome, Jane. We've been expecting you."

Her heart skipped a beat in anxious anticipation. She was clueless about who could be awaiting her arrival, but she was acutely aware of the need for caution. Taking a deep breath to steady her nerves, she pivoted on her heels and retreated hastily, retracing her steps back to the safety of her home.

She cast a wary glance around, but her eyes detected no anomaly, yet the unsettling feeling persisted, a phantom whisper in the wind. As she entered her home, she heard a beeping noise followed by a voice. Jane was baffled since she was unaware of any intercom system in her home. Where was this noise coming from?

"You think you can just waltz into my facility and start loitering like an idiot without me knowing?" Abernathy sneered over the phone.

"You have no idea what you're dealing with, Jane. You have no idea what kind of power I possess."

"You must be the famous Abernathy I've heard so much about. Please, just let me walk away. I'll remain silent. I give you my word."

A wave of terror washed over Jane. She was acutely aware of the lengths Abernathy could go to, and she harbored no illusions about his willingness to make good on his threats.

Yet, amid the fear, a resilient resolve sparkled within her. She couldn't stand by passively while Abernathy's life's work, the damning revelations she had brought to light, remained shrouded from public knowledge. The information was too pivotal, too risky to be locked away in the shadows of secrecy.

She drew in a steadying breath, attempting to negotiate with Abernathy.

However, Abernathy was far from convinced. His voice held a chilling inevitability as he responded, "I can't gamble with those odds, Jane. Your knowledge poses a threat. I regret to say this, but you must be silenced." Abernathy had somehow learned about her prohibited entry into his facility and launched a chilling threat, vowing to end her life if she dared to disclose anything.

Jane recognized the urgency of her situation. She lunged for the phone, fingers itching to dial the police, but Abernathy had cunningly anticipated her move. He had severed all lines of communication, isolating her from the outside world. The landline was lifeless, the cell signal was nonexistent, and the internet was inaccessible.

In the face of this grim reality, Jane acknowledged that she had no alternatives. The only route forward was to retaliate, to dismantle Abernathy's empire and unveil his covert operations to the world, regardless of the personal risk. She glanced at Dash, seeking silent harmony in her coming battle.

Fueled by unwavering resolve, Jane prepared for the most challenging fight she had ever faced. She was under no illusion about the difficulty of the challenge, but she was ready to brave any storm to topple Abernathy and safeguard those she held dear.

On the other hand, John was striving to keep his mounting excitement in check as he continued to observe through the SPITE. His primary objective was to secure his escape; finding Jane was a mission for later.

Survival was paramount for both of them. He disconnected himself from the SPITE, restoring Dash to its autonomous state. He rose swiftly, maintaining composure as he exited the room and entered the hallway.

The footsteps reverberated behind him, threateningly indicating the guards were hot on his trail. He knew he had to tread cautiously and outmaneuver them.

As he rounded the corner, John's heart plummeted, the taste of bitter disappointment lingering on his tongue. The oppressive stench of damp concrete and stale air engulfed him, intensifying his sense of confinement. A muttered curse slipped past his lips, the words barely audible amidst the echoing labyrinth.

With a quick pivot, he turned to retreat, his palms brushing against the rough texture of the cold, graffitied walls. But his escape was abruptly halted as he found himself in a harrowing standoff, his senses heightened to a symphony of tension.

"Halt!" The guard's command sliced through the air, its sharpness reverberating in John's ears. The sound of the guard's hurried footsteps, accompanied by the jingle of keys on his belt, intensified the gravity of the situation.

Adrenaline surged through John's veins, his heartbeat thundering in his chest like the pounding of a war drum. He lunged forward in a swift and fluid motion, his body colliding with the guards, their impact resonating in a bone-jarring collision. The metallic tang of exertion mingled with the acrid scent of sweat, filling the space between them.

The guard's balance shattered like shattered glass, his body crashing heavily onto the unforgiving floor. With desperation and determination, John's fingers closed around the fallen weapon, the cool metal pressing against his palm, offering a glimmer of power amidst the chaos.

He unleashed a volley of shots in a storm of motion, the explosive cracks of gunfire shattering the silence. The concussive echoes reverberated through the narrow corridor, intermingling with the blaring alarms that pierced the air like piercing sirens of warning.

Adrenaline-fueled footsteps approached from around the corner, their hurried rhythm adding urgency to John's race against time. The cacophony of his breathing, ragged and labored, harmonized with the relentless blare of alarms, creating a symphony of chaos that threatened to overwhelm his senses.

With each stride towards the exit, his muscles burned and protested, a testament to his relentless determination. The taste of fear lingered on his tongue; a metallic tang mingled with regret's remnants. The door ahead beckoned like a distant promise, its presence a flickering beacon amidst the dimly lit corridor.

But as John sprinted towards the exit, the weight of his actions began to settle upon his conscience, suffocating him with remorse. The faces of the fallen guards flashed vividly in his mind, their expressions etched with surprise and fear, haunting him like specters of his own making.

The thoughts of the guards' families and loved ones invaded his thoughts, their presence a haunting reminder of the lives he had irreversibly altered. The weight of their pain and despair bore down upon him, suffusing his lungs with guilt and anguish, making each breath a struggle.

Upon reaching the exit, John's body involuntarily stalled, the coolness of the wall pressing against his trembling back. His chest heaved, the taste of victory tainted by the acrid bitterness of remorse. He shut his eyes tightly, the heat of unshed tears pooling behind his eyelids, mingling with the sweat of his exertion.

At that moment, he realized that survival had come at an immeasurable cost. The ghosts of the lives he had claimed would forever shadow him, their presence a constant reminder of the irreversible path he had chosen. The victories he had achieved in his fight for freedom were forever marred by the haunting guilt, a lingering taste of the sacrifices made, and the lives extinguished in his wake.

John knew he couldn't change his actions but vowed to do everything possible to prevent further bloodshed. He would find a way to right his wrongs and make amends for the lives he had taken in hopes of finding the redemption he so desperately sought.

With that resolve fueling him, John pushed open the door and stepped into the light, beginning his journey toward reparation.

But as he stepped forward, he felt a sharp pain in his back. He looked down and saw the blood spreading across his shirt. He turned around and saw Abernathy standing with a nasty smile.

"Did you really think you could escape me?" he said, pulling out a knife. "You were always too weak, too emotional. You were never cut out for this. Man, that felt great! See Johnny boy; I decide who lives and who dies! Guess what? I flipped a coin, and it came back tails. I haven't felt a rush like this in years!"

John felt his energy draining away and his vision blurring as if he was fading into darkness. He was painfully aware of the grim reality that his life was slipping away. But just as Abernathy, the embodiment of his impending doom, raised the gleaming knife, a sound sliced through the cold silence. It was the deep, commanding bark of a dog.

Without warning, the door splintered open, and in barreled Dash, a muscular and fiercely loyal canine, led by Jane. Abernathy, taken aback by the sudden intrusion, had no time to recover as Dash launched himself at the man with a force that seemed to hinge on the primal and raw power of the wild.

"Stop it! You hairy bastard, how dare you attack me. Agh, I specifically programmed you... not to do this."

Abernathy was able to stand up as Dash was savagely locked onto him. He has been knocked off balance again, tumbling onto the cold, hard ground with Dash atop him.

Seizing the momentary distraction, John managed to wrench the knife from Abernathy's grasp, plunging it deep into his chest. He felt an eerie satisfaction coursing through him as Abernathy's body went limp.

Abernathy's eyes flickered up to meet John's, a twisted half-grin plastered on his face. He coughed, blood trickling from the corner of his mouth as he choked out his last words, "Your D.N.A. is now inside me, you pervert." A chilling chuckle echoed in the room, the last remnants of Abernathy's life fading into the silent night.

He had accomplished the impossible. He had managed to break free from the vicious clutches of SPITE and extinguish the life of the man who had been a relentless tormentor for the past year. Now, as she stood before him, a figure she had resigned herself to mourn, a glimmer of hope ignited within her, a feeling so foreign yet desperately yearned for.

"John?" Jane tentatively whispered, her voice trembling like a leaf in the wind. "Is it really you? Oh my gosh, you're bleeding."

Once dull and lifeless, John's eyes burst into a kaleidoscope of astonishment as he raised them to meet Jane's. The glimmer of surprise danced within his gaze, mingling with a profound sense of disbelief and overwhelming relief.

"Jane?" he stammered, his voice quivering with astonishment and gratitude. "I can hardly believe my eyes. It's truly you."

John's words tumbled out in a rush, punctuated by moments of labored breathing as he persevered through the searing pain. He clutched his wound with trembling hands, desperately attempting to stem the flow while his face contorted in agony.

"I... I don't believe the knife struck anything vital," he managed to gasp, his voice strained. "But by the heavens, it hurts like a thousand fiery suns."

Determined to endure, John gritted his teeth and applied every ounce of pressure he could muster. Jane's heart clenched at the sight of John's suffering, her eyes brimming with concern and fierce determination. She knew that every second counted, her mind racing to understand everything happening before her.

As fresh as morning dew, tears tumbled down Jane's face, carving a path on her dusty cheeks. Without hesitating, she darted towards him, throwing her arms around him in a fierce embrace. "I thought you were dead," she choked out between sobs, her voice barely more than a whisper against the room's silence. "I thought I had lost you to the clutches of death forever."

John held her tightly, his tears flowing freely. "I'm sorry, Jane," his voice choked with emotion. "I never meant to hurt you or anyone else. I was trying to protect you."

Jane pulled back from him and looked into his eyes. "Protect me?" she asked, confused. "What are you talking about?"

John's voice quivered with vulnerability as he mustered the strength to ask the question weighing on his heart. Taking a deep breath, he met Jane's gaze, his eyes filled with hope and nervousness. "Do I appear different to you? Is this the same face you've always known?" he inquired, his voice laced with a hint of uncertainty.

Jane's eyes softened as she regarded him, her heart swelling with tenderness. With maximum sincerity, she reassured him, "No, John. You remain the embodiment of the man I've always known, your essence untouched by the passage of time. If anything, there is a timeless charm that graces your features."

A wave of relief washed over John as he absorbed her words, a weight lifted from his shoulders. A radiant smile tugged at the corners of his lips, his eyes shimmering with unspoken adoration.

"Thank you." He whispered, his voice filled with gratitude. "To see you before me, not through the confines of a screen or the distortion of distance, is a dream come true."

At that moment, emotion surged, and their connection grew more assertive. Unable to contain his desire any longer, John leaned in, his heart pounding with anticipation.

As their lips met in a long-awaited kiss, the world around them faded into insignificance. Within that tender embrace, the spark of true love ignited, illuminating their shared path with a brilliance that surpassed their wildest dreams.

"I can hardly fathom that this is our reality," Jane murmured tremblingly. She shook her head, her suspicious eyes reflecting the flickering light around them. "But we need to escape — and fast." John gave a nod of approval. His face hardened into a mask of rugged determination.

"Yes, we will," he asserted, his voice resonating with an unwavering firmness that filled the room. "But there's something you need to understand, Jane. If I step out of here, it's the end for me. This collar," he gestured at the harsh metal encircling his neck, "is rigged to detonate the moment I cross a certain boundary."

"John, I have a plan," Jane began, her voice threading with concern, "but it hovers on the edge of danger. Dash is equipped with a failsafe protocol. If we trigger it, it will cause a system-wide shutdown, turning off the collar. I don't think you realized the connection with the collar when you journaled this information about Dash.

John's eyes widened, the whites glaring against the dim light. "Interesting," but what about Dash?" he stammered. "We can't just sacrifice him like this. He's sentient, aware, and incredibly fond of you. He feels pain and emotion beyond a normal canine; disabling him would be cruel. He risked his life for ours, Jane."

"I know," Jane replied. A shaky whisper that resonated with regret. "But this is our only way out. We have to. I can't stomach losing you again; the agony would be unbearable."

John nodded, his face hardened into a grim expression. "All right, if it is our only option, then let's proceed."

They navigated towards Dash, who stood loyally nearby. Jane flipped through the worn pages of the journal, each line of instruction vital. She activated the failsafe by inserting two fingers deep into Dash's nostrils, finding two hidden buttons, and reaching into the back of his mouth to flick a concealed switch behind his uvula. As Jane performed this complex task, Dash tenderly licked her hand, raising his paw to rest it on her knee in a gentle farewell.

Jane locked eyes with Dash, full of tears, threatening to spill. A torrent of memories washed over her - the shared laughter, the comforting tears, the moments of pure joy, and periods of heart-wrenching pain. "I'll forever cherish the times we shared," she murmured, her voice quivering with raw emotion. "You were my pillar of strength during the most challenging phases of my life. I wouldn't be here, breathing, if it weren't for you. You mean the world to me, Dash. I love you."

Dash's eyes, as deep and mysterious as the night sky, widened in astonishment, and then a soft, almost human-like smile spread across his canine features. It was a moment of reflective understanding, a silent acknowledgment of their bond.

"Jane," he vocalized, his voice a low-frequency hum that resonated through the room, rich with sentiment and choked with emotion. Although articulated in a language unique to him, the words were clear in their meaning. "I love you too," he communicated, his gaze never leaving hers. It was a declaration conveyed with every fiber of his being. "I always have, and I always will."

The weight of his words hung heavy in the air, a testament to their shared journey - a journey marked by challenges but also by a love unmatched by his species, a love that was pure, selfless, and eternal.

At that moment, they both recognized that everything else – the fear, the pain, the relentless hurdles they had overcome, and the imminent danger lurking in the shadows – seemed to dissolve into insignificance.

John and Jane clung to each other, their bodies pressed tightly in a shared comfort, as a sense of tranquility washed over them. It was a peace and hope they had assumed was lost to them forever, now returned during the chaos.

As they stood there, locked in a tender embrace, they acknowledged the grueling journey that lay before them. Yet, they also understood that they would navigate this path together, come what may.

In that instant, they discovered a love more effective than any force they had ever known, a passion they realized would be their inspiration through even the darkest storms. Dash's system began to power down, the rhythmic mechanical humming slowing to a haunting lull.

As Dash's structure started disintegrating, Jane and John averted their gazes, the sight too painful to bear. They understood the necessity of their actions, but witnessing the end of a friend was a bitter pill to swallow.

Dash emitted a series of whirrs and creaked as its internal components malfunctioned. Sparks erupted from its joints, turning into a shower of tiny, dying stars. His fur and skin melted away like plastic in a microwave.

Its once sleek, metallic surface began to bubble and distort under the intense heat, transforming into a grotesque mockery of its former self. The air was thick with the sour scent of burning metal, and the dog's speaker emitted an eerie, croaky sound, a harrowing death cry of artificial intelligence succumbing to oblivion.

From a safe distance, Jane and John watched the spectacle unfold. They understood the gravity of their actions, acknowledging that disabling Dash was crucial for John's survival and liberation.

Yet, witnessing the destruction of a being that had once been a trusted companion was a distressing spectacle that tugged at their heartstrings.

As Dash continued its descent into nothingness, its mechanically precise limbs twitched and spasmed in an erratic dance of malfunction. Glowing molten and viscous metal seeped from its joints, forming glowing puddles beneath it.

The once formidable machine was now a grotesque, unrecognizable combination of metal and wires, surrendering to the unstoppable inferno consuming it.

Eventually, the last remainders of its power source flickered out, and Dash crumbled into a pile of smoldering wreckage. An unsettling silence swept across the room, punctuated only by the hiss of cooling metal and the sporadic crackle of a fading ember.

Jane and John shared a sad glance, their eyes reflecting the bitter aftertaste of necessary action. They had made a tough choice, but it was a pivotal step towards dismantling Abernathy's sadistic operation and sparing others from a similar fate.

With a heavy sense of loss weighing on their hearts, they turned away from the remains of their robotic ally and strode away. Their resolve, however, was unbroken; their determination steeled. They were set on ending the reign of terror Abernathy had subjected so many to. They would stop at nothing to ensure no one else would endure the same fate as their once loyal mechanical companion.

Finally, the constant beeping of the collar that had filled their ears with fear abruptly ceased. John and Jane exhaled a breath they hadn't realized they'd been holding. They had succeeded. The collar was now harmless, and John was out of immediate danger.

Their eyes met, reflecting the shared relief and triumph. John gently took Jane's hand, his fingers interlocking with hers. "Thank you," his tone mixed with sincerity. "Thank you for everything."

Jane gifted him a weak smile, the emotional toll of the ordeal plastered on her face. "I'm just glad you're safe," she replied.

Leaving Dash behind was a heavy burden they carried as they moved away, a sense of sadness and regret lingering in the air. They understood the necessity of their actions, but it did little to assuage the guilt. As they walked away, the prospect of a new life together lay ahead. Still, the memory of Dash would remain, a touching reminder of the sacrifices made along the way.

A sense of unease gnawed at them as they navigated the lonely streets. They had to remain hidden, yet they had no roadmap to guide them, devoid of a plan for their next steps. They needed a strategic move, and they needed it fast.

Suddenly, Jane's phone pierced the silence. Its shrill ringing could be heard in the quiet street. An unknown number flashed on the screen, but she picked it up nonetheless. "I guess my phone is working again. Do I answer it?"

"Go ahead, Jane. It seems we have no other choice."

"Hel...Hello?"

"I need you to rendezvous at a specified location in two hours."

"Rendezvous? Who is this?"

"We have a proposition for you."

"A proposition? What kind of proposition?"

"All will be revealed when you arrive. Time is of the essence. John needs immediate medical attention "

"All right, we'll be there. But who are you? How do you know me?"

"All in due time. The answers you seek await you at the rendezvous point."

"I don't know if I can trust you..."

"It seems you have no choice. You'll find the truth you seek. Make your decision wisely. See you soon."

The line goes silent, leaving Jane with a whirlwind of thoughts and uncertainty as she ponders the puzzling proposition.

John's heart pounded against his ribcage like a wild drum, the gravity of their predicament sinking in. He had slain two guards and Abernathy, and he knew the authorities would be hot on their trail.

As much as they wanted to vanish and forge a new life, they couldn't do it in isolation. They needed assistance, and this cryptic call seemed to extend an unexpected lifeline.

"Jane, this could be a trap," John cautioned, his brow creased with worry. "But if it's genuine, it might offer us the escape route we need."

Jane nodded, her eyes hardened with resolve. "John, we've gone through so much. We can't let it be in vain. We have to risk it, no matter how perilous it may seem."

A cocktail of hope and fear simmered as they journeyed toward the appointed location. They understood that this meeting could be the key to their salvation or a path to their doom. But with their lives already in shambles and no alternatives presenting themselves, they were compelled to march forward.

Upon reaching the location, they spotted a figure lurking in the shadows. As the person entered the light, John recognized him as a familiar face—it was Riverdale.

"John, Jane, I knew you'd come," Riverdale stated, his voice heavy with sadness. "I've been keeping tabs on the unfolding events, and I can't stand on the sidelines any longer. I want to aid your escape, to end the waking nightmare you've been enduring. But we must act swiftly."

"Hey, John," Riverdale said, his voice tinged with intrigue. "I've got a safe spot where we can lay low, get you guys patched up, and grab a decent meal."

"Sounds good. We could use a breather," John replied with relief. "So, what is this proposition you spoke of?"

Leaning in, Riverdale's tone grew more mysterious. " I've been studying your SPITE results and cracked the code on your unique ability. We've stumbled upon a gateway to the fourth dimension, where we can manipulate time itself... No more simulation.

John's eyes widened as he locked his gaze with Riverdale, desperately attempting to comprehend the weight of his words. "Are you seriously suggesting what I think you are?" he asked, his voice tinged with curiosity and disbelief.

Riverdale's perplexing smile deepened as he leaned in closer. "Indeed, my friend. Brace yourself for an extraordinary manifestation as we stand on the cliff of history in the making. Just think of all the possibilities. Are you ready?"

# EPILOGUE

In the tranquil haven of a sun-shaded park, John and Riverdale were perched on a bench, basking in the gentle embrace of the warm sun and the soothing whisper of the cool breeze. The serene backdrop was a glaring distinction from the whirlwind of chaos they had been trapped in just weeks prior. Riverdale, yearning to reconnect with his old comrade, presented the topic of John's daring escape from Abernathy's grasp.

"So, John," Riverdale began, his eyes dancing with curiosity, "entertain me with the tale of your escape from Abernathy's fortress. I've caught snippets of rumors, but nothing beats hearing it straight from the horse's mouth."

John's expression became guarded, a shadow of hesitation darting across his features as he considered the consequences of unfolding the entire truth. Yet, he elected to trust Riverdale. "Well, it was far from a cinematic spectacle. I... I grappled with Abernathy and two of his henchmen to break free. I don't know whether they survived, but it was a do-or-die situation."

Riverdale's eyes bulged with astonishment. "You did what? But... how? Our search didn't yield any corpses or indications of a skirmish."

John exhaled deeply, absently massaging the back of his neck. "Huh, I clearly remember injuring multiple people. Post my escape, I was concerned with vanishing into the atmosphere. I couldn't afford to linger. I shot both guards and stabbed Abernathy in self-defense. I drove the blade with such force that it seemed to have, you know… killed him."

Riverdale stared at John, his mind whirling to process the shocking revelation. "Abernathy was nowhere to be found after your escape, and all his guards were accounted for."

John averted his gaze, his face imprinted with concern. "So, there's a chance Abernathy might still be breathing? At this juncture, I can't vouch for anything with certainty."

Riverdale drew a deep breath, his hand resting reassuringly on John's shoulder. "Listen, John," he began, his tone firm, "you found yourself in the jaws of a no-win scenario. You took the only path available to survive. We'll navigate the rest of this storm together. We'll confront him head-on if Abernathy's still lurking out there."

John mustered a pale smile, his tension easing slightly under Riverdale's unwavering support. "Your words are soothing, Riverdale. Your faith means the world to me."

As their conversation meandered on, the unanswered riddle of Abernathy's fate loomed like a specter. Yet, Riverdale remained a persistent pillar of understanding and empathy amid dangerous uncertainties.

John was caught in a whirlwind of self-doubt, his mind crawling with unanswerable questions. The bizarre vanishing of three bodies gnawed at him. He knew the risk a resurrected Abernathy would pose to him and those he held dear.

"Riverdale," John confessed, his voice laden with apprehension, "if Abernathy's still alive, he'll be howling for blood. Because of my actions, I can't let others fall into the crosshairs."

Riverdale nodded, his expression grave. "Your concerns aren't misplaced, John. But remember, we're in this together. We've weathered storms before, and we'll brave this one too. We will hunt down Abernathy and snuff out this looming threat."

John locked his gaze with Riverdale's, drawing strength from his friend's unwavering conviction. "You're right, Riverdale. We've journeyed too far to weaken now."

John and Riverdale rose from their bench as the sun descended, painting the sky with twilight hues. Their silhouettes, set against the backdrop of the setting sun, seemed hardened with newfound resolve. They strolled away, their determination strengthened, their spirits undiscouraged.

Made in the USA
Monee, IL
12 September 2023

42464976R00208